THE DEATH KNOT

CAROLYN BANKS

The Death Knot

Edited by Lisa Diane Kastner

Published in North America and Europe by Running Wild Press. Visit Running Wild Press at www.runningwildpublishing.com. Educators, librarians, book clubs (as well as the eternally curious), go to www.runningwildpublishing.com.

Paperback ISBN: 978-1-963869-36-1
eBook ISBN: 978-1-963869-37-8

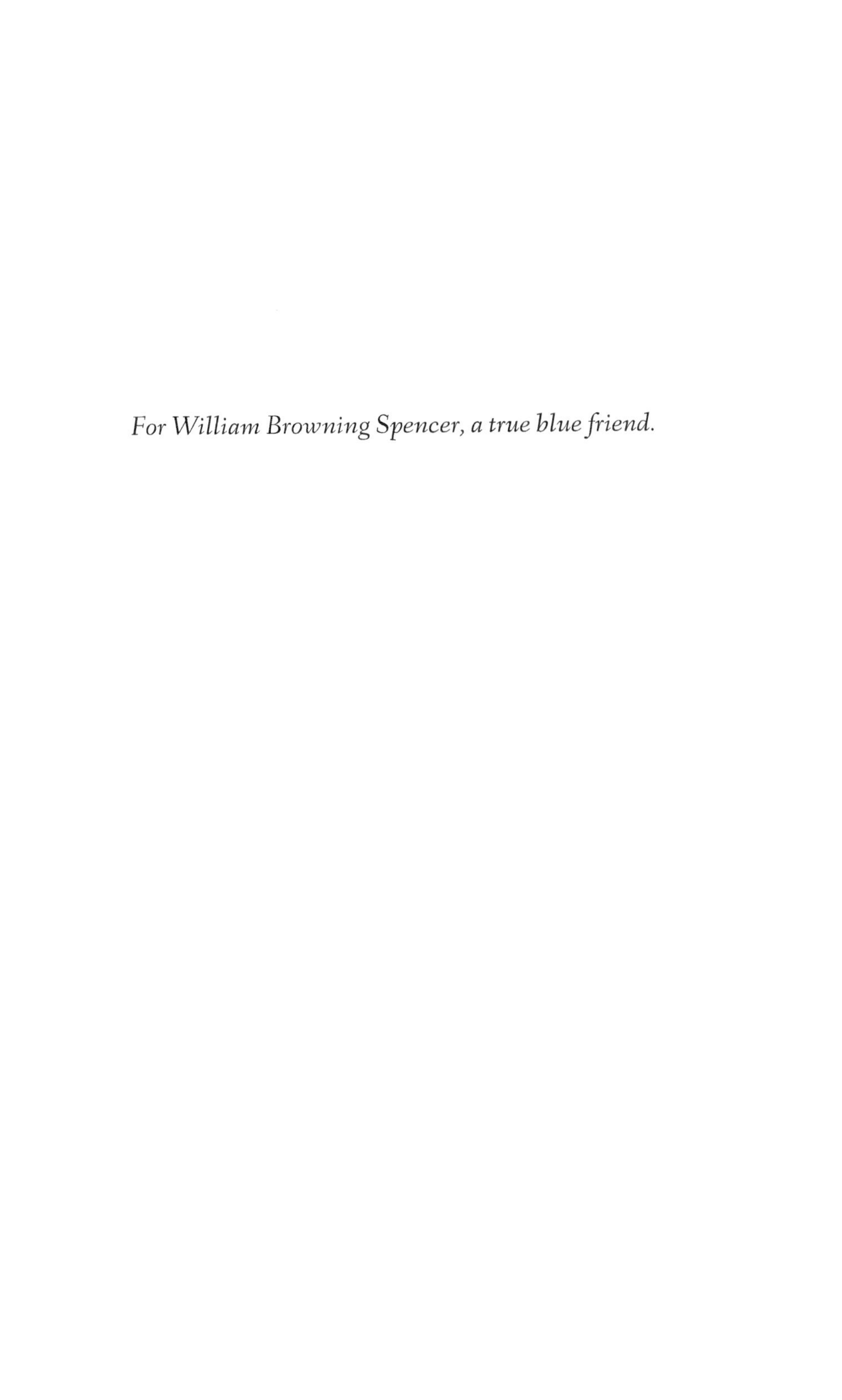

For William Browning Spencer, a true blue friend.

CHAPTER ONE

Before the murders, I was just sort of waiting to die. I wasn't terminally ill and I certainly wasn't suicidal, but there was nothing going on in my life, nothing to keep me interested.

I slept a lot. I ate far too much. I didn't read anymore. I watched a lot of television, bouncing from HGTV home makeovers to violent crime, *Chicago P.D.* and *Law and Order* reruns, mostly.

I could still manage to do the work I do, selecting textiles for a clothing designer, but I worked at home, mostly. My job required that I traveled occasionally, but I always did that alone. I liked that I had pretty much sequestered myself from human contact.

My doctor didn't think it was quite the blessing that I felt it was and prescribed an antidepressant, Citalopram, and insisted that I walk at least half an hour every day. I said I would do that, and that is how the whole thing began, with me getting into my car and driving to the park less than a mile away to walk along the path that flanked the river. The path was known throughout Lost Pines as the Riverwalk.

I never meant to talk to anyone, much less befriend anyone. But being there every day at approximately the same time meant that a "Hello" or a "Good morning" would be called for.

And if I were seen parking my car, a 2001 Mercedes roadster, I attracted a lot of attention—everything from "Nice ride" to "What's it got?" I'm 49 years old. That means I had just turned 31 when the car was manufactured, but it was so well kept that it looked brand new. The truth is, I felt younger than 31 when I was driving the car. I felt 21, pretty and sassy and beautifully dressed. I hadn't become the loner that I am now and that I have been for at least two years.

Anyway, my car. I don't know diddly about cars. I bought this one used from a classified ad. I liked that it was a two-seater and, even though it was a hard top, I could push a button on the console and, like magic, the roof would rise and disappear into the trunk. I wouldn't have imagined being in a teeny car with the Texas roads full of huge pickup trucks, but the car alleviated all my fears. If a truck comes, I hit the gas and zoom away. Hit the gas and zoom away was pretty much my current philosophy.

At the Riverwalk parking lot I would display the engine of the car rather than answer the questions about the engine and wait to hear what it was I had. The funny thing is that, in my car at least, there's some kind of plate between the engine and the viewer. No one seemed to be daunted by this. And, I should add that those viewing the engine seldom said the same thing.

Men.

But anyway, except for the brief excitement of flooring Slick (Well, yes, I named the car but it was only so I could remember what it was, an SLK 320) I trudged through my days, walked in the mornings, ate when I got home and then napped, usually. It wasn't much of a life and I was all too aware of that.

The isolation was most pronounced before, during and after Christmas and New Year's Day, when nothing was required of me by the designer I worked for. These days were the slowest. My awareness of how totally I'd separated myself from the world around me was heightened when everyone else was buying and wrapping presents and attending holiday parties.

But all of that, everything, changed with the first murder.

DECEMBER 21, 2019

The barking dog didn't register until I'd rounded the bend in the path. It was a Jack Russell Terrier I knew as Sadie. There she was, her leash dragging, barking at her owner, Farley Clement.

Farley was hunched over the body of a person larger than himself. He was beating the person with his cane, beating him with force I never dreamed a man Farley's age--in his late seventies at least--could muster.

The noises--Sadie yapping, Farley grunting and the wet, pulpy sound of every blow--are something I hope I will one day forget.

The sight was made even more bizarre by the Christmas decorations that lined either side of the walkway. An angel held a trumpet to the sky. A huge styrofoam snowman in a Santa hat waved. A sign proclaiming PEACE ON EARTH flashed off and on, strobing the murder scene.

The face of the victim was turned to the side so that he appeared to be looking at me. He seemed to be smiling. The blows had destroyed the back of his head and his neck, but his face, eyes opened and mouth quirked into an odd smile, was intact.

Farley's eyes, the eyes of the murderer, bulged, wide open. His glasses were half off, just hanging there from one ear. He was spotted with blood and what had to be pieces of human tissue.

Maybe it isn't Farley, I hoped, but of course it was, his thick wooden cane, his navy blue cardigan, white shirt and red bow tie.

I don't know how long I'd been standing there, but a voice behind me jarred me out of my paralysis.

"Stay back," the voice said, and its burly owner, Carl, I think, walked toward Farley and his victim. Carl held his cell phone in front of himself like a shield as he recorded Farley's last, much-weakened blows. Then I saw Carl aim the phone downward, to get a shot of the victim's body.

By now, three or four other walkers had amassed. I heard someone offer to call 911. Sadie, Farley's dog, wandered through the legs of the people and finally came to me. Absentmindedly, I picked up her leash.

I made out a few words of the bystander's 911 call. "Accident...Riverwalk...down past the bridge."

Accident?

I stepped to where I could see Farley again. He was on his knees and leaning back on his haunches, holding his hands up in the air and looking quizzically at them. They were wildly misshapen, swollen and twisted, as though he'd removed them and put them back incorrectly.

Farley was spattered with blood and gunk. His face had lost its former fierce appearance so completely that I wondered if that had been something I imagined rather than saw. Those bulging eyes, the heartless curl of his mouth.

The cane had cracked in half. Part of it lay near Farley's knees and the other half, the top of it, a piece of wood carved into the shape of a duck's head, was on the other side of the body.

We all kind of backed away, though we continued to stare. I looked around. Yes, all eyes were on Farley and the person he had killed.

Carl spoke to Farley, loud enough so we all could hear. "We're gonna get you some help, man. Don't you worry none." Carl timidly leaned over the body and touched Farley's arm for a second before turning to address us, a crowd of about eight now. "I don't guess any of us ought to leave."

Sadie tugged the leash, trying to persuade me to disobey. She appeared to have forgotten all about her owner and was bent on her morning walk.

Farley continued examining his hands, first one, then the other, the palms, then the tops. They were blood-soaked, huge and puffy, with fingers pointing ways they really didn't. He had broken his hands, clearly, by delivering the blows.

"Carl," I tapped his shoulder. He seemed to be in charge. I gestured at the body on the ground in front of Farley. A young person with an unlined, slightly quizzical face who wore tattered jeans, brand new athletic shoes, and a backpack. "Who?" I whispered. It appeared to be a boy. A boy with the back of his skull quite gone.

"I know as much as you do," Carl said, "which is nada. But I think we ought to just be quiet until the police get here."

"But what about Farley?" I asked.

"Just let him be. We don't want to rile him up again."

And so, for what seemed a very long time, Farley, looking slightly stunned, knelt at the side of his victim, while the crowd of people at the scene of the murder grew. We all knew with a brief glance there was nothing we could do to help the boy. What had been the back of his head had been battered beyond the reach of medicine. And Farley, well, if my own feelings were any indication, we were all feeling kind of sorry for him.

"Kid must have jumped him," someone offered.

"And he got his," another man said, with a half-laugh. Everyone made the same sound of assent at the notion of Farley, the victim of a would-be mugging, delivering a fate this severe.

And then the police were there, all of them painfully young and looking as stunned as we had when we'd first come upon the scene.

They took names, addresses, phone and email information, though not in any orderly fashion. They said they'd be in touch. Then a pair of cops got on either side of Farley and helped him to his feet. Farley had to lean on one of them fairly heavily in order to stand. The police were patient. They let Farley get his bearings once he was standing, then gently nudged him so that he turned away from the boy he had killed.

They began to guide Farley toward the long steep flight of stairs that led to a parking lot at this end of the park. Farley seemed puzzled but went with them. He was shuffling, as though it was painful to walk.

Sadie wanted to accompany Farley now, but another policeman stopped me. "We're putting him in an ambulance," the policeman explained. "We'll take him to Austin, Stoneridge, treat those hands of his. Then, I don't know what."

"This kid must have tried to attack him or something," I said.

Carl handed his cell phone over to the cop. It was covered in camouflage fabric, matching the clothing Carl nearly always wore. The cop nodded toward Carl. "I'll get you a receipt for this," the cop said. "We'll get it back to you."

"It's all there," Carl said.

A thought about the monetary value of the footage on the cell phone flitted through my head and it embarrassed me to think that way. But hadn't Mr. Zabruder been paid for the JFK assassination footage? I'd heard that somewhere. I felt my face turning red. Then I realized Carl had arrived at the scene after I had. He couldn't possibly have captured what had happened beginning to end.

"You want to sit down somewhere?" the cop asked me. "We can go to that bench over there." Without waiting for a response, he steered me to the bench.

"The old man, his name's Farley Clement, is that right?" the cop asked.

"Yes. He was pretty well known in town." I don't even know how I knew this. Walking on the Riverwalk regularly as I now do, I just picked stuff up. I knew that he had been a popular high school teacher and had retired.

I answered all of the cop's questions. My name, address and such. Although I was holding Sadie's leash and she was indicating impatience, I wasn't asked about Farley's dog. I guess it was assumed the dog was mine.

The policeman turned around and noticed that Farley and the other cops had just finished making their ascent up the staircase. It was almost as if the cop talking to me didn't want to be left behind. "You take care," he said. He flipped his notepad shut, stood, and abruptly moved off. Meanwhile, another crew headed down the stairs, this one seemingly medical, consisting of five men and a woman carrying bags and odd pieces of equipment and a very important-looking camera. They surrounded the boy's body, but from a distance and one of them stepped very close to the corpse with a camera. I could hear the *click click click* and then the camera person left and the rest of the team began working on some part of the crime scene.

I looked down at Sadie, who was wagging her tail. I started to move away from what I gathered was the forensic team and turned back down the winding riverside path. The other bystanders, Carl included, had disappeared. "I think I know where you live," I told the dog. I waited as she sniffed a pile of leaves.

I was about to pull her away when I noticed she'd unearthed something. I reached down and found, yes, a cell phone.

I brushed away the debris that was on it. It was a black leather case with a white skull imprinted on it.

I looked back at the people working on the crime scene. The place where I was standing was not terribly far from the spot where the boy's life ended. And wouldn't a skull be the sort of art that a teen might favor?

I started towards the forensic team with the phone in my outstretched hand. A young woman dressed in a police uniform that seemed way too tight for her turned in my direction. I opened my mouth to speak, but her face, which had been neutral, coiled into a scowl.

"Get back," she said. "And put that phone away."

I took another step forward.

The woman grabbed the officer next to her and he, too, looked at me with the same threatening demeanor. He moved closer to the woman and said something and then they both put their hands on their hips in defiance. It was a pose that was meant to back me up and make me do what the female officer had said.

"All right." I said, thrusting the phone into my pocket. "I'm leaving." *Screw them.*

I heard the female officer say, "some people," as though my attempt put me in the company of ghouls who liked to photograph gory scenes.

I walked back towards the parking lot, passed a makeshift stable where Mary, Joseph and three wise men hovered over the baby Jesus. Inwardly, I was fuming. I may have been handing the police important evidence, and they had not allowed it to happen; they had not taken me seriously.

I felt my anger rise. Again, *Screw them!*

Along the route back to my car, I passed a lot of the regulars and said 'Good morning' as usual. No one seemed to think it odd that I had a dog with me, especially since the dog was Sadie, Farley's dog, a dog that many knew by name.

And the people I passed seemed not to know about the drama that had transpired on the far end of the path. It was just as well.

When I got to my car, Sadie hesitated momentarily, then leapt over the center console into the passenger seat. She was used to being in a vehicle, I noted. She looked over at me as if eager to get going. I wondered if Farley had a sports car too, since Sadie seemed comfortable and ready. I backed out and turned to head up Wilder.

At the stop sign on Main, I noticed a couple in a black SUV, a Cadillac Escalade heading toward the park. The woman was crying, looking out the window on the passenger side. The man was red-faced, arguing with her or lecturing her about something. And instantly the thought popped into my head: *The dead kid's parents.*

I forced myself to ignore the thought and keep driving. After all, even if my suspicion was correct, I could hardly interrupt the couple to ask if it could possibly be their son I had just seen murdered. But something about the certainty I'd felt when I saw them unsettled me. That's who they were all right.

If it weren't for the huge, silver, older model American car in the driveway, Farley and Leona's house would have seemed uninhabited. A rural mailbox with junk mail bulged from it and quite a few pieces were on the ground. The walkway was concrete with holes and cracks and crooked spots, far beyond repair. There was no lawn to speak of, just a brown bed of tall, bristly weeds.

The front door was one of those old-fashioned aluminum storm doors. The wooden door beyond it was wide open so that I could see inside to the dark interior.

I knocked on the aluminum door and could see someone coming from within the house. Just before she reached me, she bent to pick something up. When she came to the door, I saw that she had picked up a dog toy in the shape of a foot. Three of the five toes had been bitten off. The remaining two were made to look as though they'd been painted with bright red nail polish. For some reason, I was revolted by it.

Leona opened the door and took Sadie's leash and closed the door again. I stood on the threshold, puzzled, as Leona and I stared at each other through the glass.

Leona was pale and thin, with stringy gray hair tied back. She wore a nightgown but had thrown what looked like a man's bathrobe over it. I thought she looked familiar, but immediately knew why: she resembled the woman in Grant Wood's painting, "American Gothic."

I wondered how I appeared to her. I had layered myself as

usual, and had recently trimmed my hair, so I looked a bit less wild than I had a week ago. I wore exquisite fabrics, but I didn't think Leona would realize that. My shoes were fashionably clunky. So maybe I looked a little too sophisticated, out of place for Lost Pines. I probably should mention that many in the past have admired my high cheekbones and thickly lashed eyes, merely a product of heredity. These physical traits, however, have caused many to say that I am beautiful.

I realized Leona was waiting for me to speak. "Your husband," I said, trying to raise my voice to make certain she could hear it. "Your husband is..."

Leona held up her hand to stop me from saying the rest. She pushed the storm door open and I took the cue and entered. She bent down to take Sadie's leash off and hung it on a hook near the door jamb. She handed the mangled foot to the dog, who took it in her jaws, moved swiftly past Leona's feet and carried it deep inside the Clement home.

"She loves that thing," Leona explained.

It smelled in there, as though the house had been closed for a long, long time. I no sooner thought it than adjusted to it, aware of it no more.

"I'm Leona Clement," she said. "It looks like Sadie got away from Farley again."

"Yes," I said.

"Well, I'm glad you knew where to bring her."

I nodded, wondering what I should say.

"Come look at something," Leona offered, rustling off ahead of me. Inside the darkened living room, she grabbed a thick electrical cord and bent, moving a curtain aside. Suddenly and incongruously, a Christmas tree overloaded with ornaments, dangling silver icicles, and bright gold tinsel lit up on the far wall.

"There," Leona said. "Merry Christmas."

"Thank you," I said. "I think I should explain...I brought your dog because your husband is...hurt. He hurt his hands. The police came..."

"Farley?" she asked. Her mouth hung open and her face puckered.

I nodded, yes.

"He's all right," I assured her. "They took him to Austin."

Leona drew a breath and clutched her heart. "Austin!" she gasped. She said it as if it were Istanbul or some other faraway place.

"They took him to Austin," I repeated. "To Stoneridge." A local hospital that anyone from here would know.

"Let's sit down," Leona said, walking over to a chair. I sat in another one just like it and faced her. "That's why you had Sadie," she said. She seemed pleased to have made this connection.

"Yes."

"And when will Farley be home?" she asked.

"I think you'll have to call someone," I said, not knowing what else to do. I wondered if she and Farley had children. A son or a daughter who could command the situation.

When I asked her, she looked wistful. "Children? There are certain children, of course. Farley's special children. But none of them truly ours." She gestured at a piece of furniture I believe is called a secretary. A glass-doored cabinet with a fancy curlique on top of a slanted piece of wood that folded out into a desk. Then Leona seemed to fall into a reverie; a smile appeared on her face. "Farley can explain it to you. He has a briefcase in that desk. I could show it to you if you have the time."

She seemed to be deliberately taking the conversation off the track. I steered it back. "The Lost Pines police," I said. "They were there. You could call them. You could call 911."

She looked hard at me.

"His hands were broken," I said. "Both of them. His cane was broken. He couldn't hold on to Sadie and that's why I had her. The police should be calling you." *Screw the police*, I thought. *Why was I here? Where were they?*

I stood up and turned towards the door. "There was an altercation," I said. I kept moving, relieved when Leona rushed off in the opposite direction. But as I reached the door, there she was, popping out of another opening in the hall.

We were about the same height. She looked deep into my eyes and placed a hand on my upper arm. "Tell me everything, dear," she said. Her breath was sour. I carefully forced myself not to jerk away and hurt her feelings. She continued, "I want to know. I need to know."

"I think someone tried to hurt Farley and he fought back," I told her. "He hurt his hands defending himself, but he's all right." I had to work at slowing the words as they came from my mouth. For a minute, I thought of blurting out the explanation, pushing her aside and making a run for my car.

She dropped her hold on me and that made me a bit less afraid.

"Call the police," I said, my voice as soft and steady as I could make it. I felt that if she knew how panicked I felt, she would get panicky too.

After a hideously long moment, she stepped back. I banged against the door to open it. It was all I could do to keep from running full speed to my car. I heard the clatter of the aluminum door shutting, then the thud of the heavy wooden door behind it.

I had the sense that the moment she saw me she suspected something bad had happened but didn't have the courage to hear it. That was what showing me the tree was all about, a delaying tactic. Talking about Farley's special children—students, I presumed—was the only time during the whole visit that she had smiled.

CHAPTER TWO

I am usually happy that I live alone, but today I was afraid to go back to my house. I drove and drove, up one street and down the next, wondering what to do. I eventually ended up at the police department, and it was there that I saw the Escalade again.

The couple was still in it, and the woman had stopped crying. Her face, like her husband's, was contorted in anger.

I walked toward their SUV, feeling as though I was fulfilling some sort of duty. Though their windows were up, I made out what they were saying as I grew near.

"Is that really what you want?" the man shouted. "Is it?"

"I don't know what I want," the woman yelled back, and then she started screaming without words, a long, wounded sound that meant she'd exhausted the expressions of pain that language could convey.

She stopped screaming when she finally heard my fist bang on the passenger side window.

So now they both stared at me, and neither seemed happy to have been interrupted.

"My name is Eleanor Armitage," I tried. "I was in the park this morning when a teenage boy got hurt."

The woman gasped. The window on her side came down.

The man slapped the steering wheel and said, "all right, dammit. All right. Let's go inside."

The woman got out of the Escalade. For a moment she seemed suspended above me, as if on a trapeze. Then she lowered herself to the pavement. She was a few inches shy of my height. She put her arms around my neck and her head on my chest and started sobbing.

Without thinking, I closed my arms around her heaving back. I felt as though I was holding her upright.

The man came around the SUV and loomed over us. Then he tried to pry his wife's arms from around my neck. "For Christ's sake, Janice," he whispered, "You're really losing it."

She pulled herself away and yelled up at him. "No!" she said. "I want to know! We have a right to know!"

And then they both bore down on me, the man's eyes hard and angry and the woman's eyes pathetic and rimmed with tears.

"It may not be your son," I said, but somehow, I knew that it was. "But a boy was hurt in the park this morning."

The woman reached for me again, but the man grabbed her and propelled her passed me up the walkway to the front door.

"What the fuck does she know?" he told his wife.

What *do* I know, really? This morning, when I got out of bed, I was just a regular person. It was four days before Christmas, and I'd been walking on the Riverwalk every morning for about a year.

The doctor had been right. During my walks, I knew I was alive.

It was a wonderful place, a place where I didn't have to think. There were geese and sometimes deer. In fact, just the other day I'd seen a deer swim across the river! And then, almost always, there were turtles on logs that had fallen in the water, all their bodies aligned, their heads craned toward the sun. If the water was especially still, I could sometimes see schools of fish, black blobs of varying lengths moving beneath the brown river surface.

And there were ducks, all kinds, white ducks, mottled ducks, ducks that looked like decoys, green heads, brown bodies. There was one duck that I especially admired, a duck that had discovered a drainage pipe that led to a sewer some twenty feet away from its entrance on the river shore. The pipe was narrow, so that, embarking on this adventure for the first time, the duck would not have been able to turn around until she'd reached the sewer itself. A very brave duck to have waddled into that long black tunnel that seemed to offer no escape. What had prompted her to try?

Anyway, but for the puzzling behavior of this one unique duck, going to the Riverwalk had been more than just physical exercise. It had been an escape, a walk into wide-eyed wonderment. I thought of a Rousseau jungle painting, prelapsarian innocence that I feared would now be tainted forever by the battering I'd witnessed at Farley Clement's hands. The sound of the blows. The blood.

At the same time, I couldn't help but question what I'd encountered. Had the boy really attempted to rob Farley? Had Farley been frightened?

On the other hand, why would anyone try to rob a walker? No one ventured to the Riverwalk with anything of value. Half the time I drove there without even a drivers' license.

But maybe that was just me and I was somehow peculiar.

I thought of the people I encountered. Not a single woman carried a purse. Maybe one or two wore a fanny pack.

No, the Lost Pines Riverwalk was not a likely spot for a profitable robbery, if that was what the murdered boy had intended.

. . .

"Come with me, please?"

The woman's voice jarred me back to the present. She had broken away from her husband and stood beside me. Her husband stood near the police station door. He glared at me, but he seemed resigned to having me along.

The woman slid her arm through mine and clutched me. The two of us walked toward the man, defying him together, sudden sisters.

No one was at the window where we might have explained our presence. The man strode to a swinging door and opened it wide. Three of the officers I'd seen at the crime scene had been talking and they all stopped and gawked at us.

One of the officers recognized me and told his fellows, "She was there. Remember?"

The three of us were escorted into what seemed to be a training room set up for an audience with a white screen erected in the front. We sat in the back row with the wife to my left, me in the middle, and the man at the end of the row.

One of the officers spoke into a device on his shoulder. "Yes, sir," he said. "They're here right now."

The husband leaned across me. "Show him the picture," he told his wife.

I thought of the cell phone in my pocket but didn't move a hand toward it. I felt my face flush.

She fished in her handbag and handed me one of those school photographs parents get every year, a package with big ones, medium sized ones and a bunch of small ones that you never knew what to do with.

I took the picture from her and stared at the kid. Yes, this was the boy. The color of his hair, maybe, or the old-fashioned way it was cut. Or just the dread that emanated from his mother, palpable in the room.

"This is our son, Brandon," the boy's mother said.

"Wait here," the policeman said, taking the photo with him.

"Jesus sweet age Christ," the man said. The boy's mother snuffled, trying not to let us know that tears had struck again.

"I can't help it, Ray. I can't," she apologized.

I felt trapped. Had I been back in my own home, I would have been in bed, the back propped up and the television on the home improvement channel, HGTV.

A large man, uniformed like the others, came into the room. He cleared his throat and stood at the end of the row. He held up the photo, his eyes fixed on the man. "Are you the father of this boy, sir?"

The man grimaced. "Raymond Sterling," he said.

"And which of you is the mother?"

Janice started wailing.

"That's my wife, Janice," Raymond said, his words tinged with disgust.

I wish I hadn't been between them. I pushed my chair back and stood, thinking that if I weren't in the way, the man would take his wife in his arms, comfort her, but that didn't happen.

The man just stared and Janice sat where she was, alternately sobbing and keening.

"I'm very sorry," the officer said, walking toward the three of us. "I'll have someone take you into Travis County to make an identification."

"Is he...?" the woman couldn't say the word.

"Yes'm. The boy in question is deceased."

With that he lowered his head and left the room.

Janice stood up and whirled around. "What is he talking about?" she yelled at me. "What do you know?" She reached for me, but her husband grabbed her wrists, knocking the chair behind him down in the process.

I backed away.

Two young cops came into the room, but neither addressed the skirmish, the upturned chair, the hollering mother. "We have a car outside," one of them said, and the two police walked passed us through the swinging doors toward the parking lot.

Janice was still intent upon me. "I want to know," she said, her voice steely, even menacing.

"There was a fight on the Riverwalk," I said. "I think your son was..." I groped for words. "Your boy was severely injured," I said, the image of the damage Farley's cane had wrought came fresh into my mind. "He was killed."

One of the younger cops came back in and held the swinging door to the side. He looked at Janice. "Ma'am. The captain thinks it would be better if we drove you there, so please, if you will."

"Where?" Janice asked.

The cop looked down at the floor. "Travis County Medical Examiner's Office."

In other words, the morgue.

I watched them go, relieved to be apart from them. I waited where I was, hoping to make certain that the police car had carried them away before I went back outside into the parking lot.

But a part of me wanted to know more. Not just about Farley and about his wife, Leona. About why all this had happened. I even wanted to know about Janice and her husband Ray, and Brandon, the dead boy.

For a moment, like a shiver, curiosity tingled through my body. I was excited, I suppose. I wasn't accustomed to the sensation.

The aftermath of the violence was strange, too. I'd never seen Janice and Ray before, and yet I'd known who they were the minute I'd laid eyes on them. I knew, too, that they didn't live in Lost Pines. It was an odd kind of knowing.

That weird sense of knowing had happened, too, when I'd asked Leona if she and Farley had children. When she'd said that thing about certain children. Certain children. What did she mean? And why had I felt a physical reaction to what she'd said. Had it been the way her eyes seemed drawn to something far away? And that smile! The smile that had crept over her face. It was as if she had a great big secret, something she and her husband shared, and the people outside the two of them be damned. Outsiders would never know. They would never guess. It was hers and Farley's and there was no stronger bond.

CHAPTER THREE

The morning walk along the river was about as social as I get. I do not know what they think they know about me, but Lost Pines is small enough for a person to develop a certain reputation and I was probably thought of as an oddity, if not crazy.

I did not know Farley in any real sense. He was one of the many I regularly encountered. He was far more formally dressed than the others. I remember thinking there was something professorial about his appearance.

The way we first met was because of his dog, Sadie. He had tied Sadie's leash to the arm of a metal bench, and he sat there, eating slices of apple out of a small plastic bag. Sadie, unbeknownst to Farley, had untied her leash and wandered down the lane toward me. I recognized what had happened and stepped on the leash, then bent down and picked it up.

When I approached Farley with the recaptured dog, he seemed unconcerned that she had broken free. He retied the leash and thanked me. "I guess she would have gone home," he said. "We live along here. You know the house with the big terraces down to the river?"

"Oh!" I said, impressed.

"Well, that's not the one. We live beside that house. You can barely see our place. Anyway, that's where Sadie was headed, I'm sure. Back to Leona, my wife. Leona was talking about baking when I left and I'm sure Sadie remembered that. Leona makes these great big gingerbread men every Christmas and we..."

I tuned out. I don't know if you've ever been trapped by an old person on a conversational roll, but they all seem to have learned the technique of talking without pause, which makes escaping difficult. I had been taught not to walk away while someone is talking and they all seem to know it, so they don't take a single breath, don't give you a chance to say, "Excuse me," and get the hell out of there.

This hadn't happened to me often, but enough for me to know the drill. I stood there with glazed eyes and waited for his monologue to end.

"I'm Farley Clement," he said at the end. "Used to teach science at the high school."

"Pleased to meet you," I said, touching his hand very briefly. Then I scurried off, resolving never to allow myself to be cornered by him again.

"Science, ha!" he called out as I walked away. "That's a good one."

I smirked, realizing that he hadn't asked, nor had I given him, *my* name. Like most older people, he was totally self-involved. I remembered thinking that he probably recorded everything about his day in a notebook, what he'd eaten, how many bowel movements he'd had.

Now, not against my better judgment but exercising no judgment at all, I walked back into the police station, searching for someone to whom I might turn over the cell phone I'd found or, better yet, someone who could provide answers.

. . .

I'll say this for the Lost Pines Police station: it is whistle clean. In fact, it looked brand spanking new, awaiting habitation. The vinyl floors gleamed. Every bit of glass was smudge—and fingerprint-free. Desks in various offices had no papers or files or artifacts upon them whatsoever.

And there were no people anywhere. Where had everyone gone?

I found myself—if watching *Law & Order* or *The Closer* on television counted for anything—in what must have been a room where suspects were interviewed. There was a table, two chairs, and a long mirror—probably a one-way mirror—on one wall.

I was irritated. Maybe even angry. Where were the police? I had someone's cell phone—perhaps the victim's—and there was no one to whom I could give it, no one who would thank me or so much as care.

Once again, the scene on the Riverwalk—the one where the forensic person and that other cop had snubbed me—came to mind. I felt my mouth tighten. Where were the goddam police?

I didn't recognize any of the cops I'd seen so far, as though a squad of new recruits had been hired. The cops I used to see were older, but just as aloof as these and, like them, a little nasty, too. I always felt as though I'd hate to have to rely on any of them for help. The deserted police station told me I'd been right.

As I approached a long hallway, I heard them. Every single one of them had been gathered in a room toward the back. As I neared it, I could see into it through a large window. Although their voices were muted by the walls, the window, and the door, most of them were clustered together singing "Jingle Bells."

Unlike the rest of the building, the room they were in had been festooned with red and green decorations. There was an enormous punchbowl, a half-eaten fruitcake, and various plates filled with cookies.

I pressed my hand against the fabric of my jacket so that I could feel the phone.

The hell with it. The phone was probably nothing. It didn't necessarily belong to the boy. As for the police, the hell with them, too.

I turned to leave just as they sang, "Ah-ha-ha-ha, Ah-ha-ha-ha," before the chorus began anew.

I imagined myself testifying at a trial. "I tried to return the phone several times, your honor, but I was ignored, rebuffed. I tried several times, but even when I made a special trip to the police station, no one was even there." That would get them. No one was even there! And indeed, I was able to leave the building without having been seen.

There must have been fourteen of Lost Pines' finest in there, and not a one had noticed me.

The SUV that the parents of the murdered boy had driven was still in the parking lot. I fished through the side pocket of my car, found an old ballpoint pen, and wrote their license plate number down on the side of a map. I had no idea how I'd use this information, but it seemed important to have it.

When I pulled up in front of my house, I was completely mystified by what I'd seen and what I'd done. For the first time in many moons, I wished I had someone to talk to.

CHAPTER FOUR

Once home, I took the phone out and stared at it. If the boy had tried to attack Farley, the attempt to get information would get him off the hook. On the other hand, I couldn't get what I'd witnessed out of my mind, so why would I want to see it again or see even more?

The sound of the blows Farley had delivered, so terrible, like—I know this sounds strange—but like the plopping of overripe apples falling in an orchard.

I shivered as I remembered that terrible sound.

The reaction of the crowd, too, was disturbing. No one tried to stop Farley, though we all could tell the boy he was hitting was already dead. We were spellbound, really. Spellbound, at least momentarily. Carl was the only one who seemed able to marshal a semblance of intelligence. If Carl hadn't been there, we'd probably still be frozen at the scene.

The cell phone. I had to look at whatever the cell phone held. But I knew nothing about cell phones. Suppose there was critical evidence on it and I inadvertently erased it? Wasn't there some way of transferring whatever the phone contained to a computer so that couldn't happen?

It was near two in the afternoon. I tried to construct a chronology. At 10 a.m. or so, I'd witnessed Farley killing an unidentified teenage boy. At about 11—had it been? returned Farley's dog to Leona, his wife. After that, I drove around. I found the parents of the boy (and I had no doubt about that, though if you asked me to cite details that proved it, I wouldn't have been able to do so) and entered the police station with them. We'd been there for 20 minutes or half an hour at the most. The police had whisked them away. And now, perhaps four hours after I'd initially left the house, I had not only seen a murder committed, but I'd pocketed what might be crucial evidence in the murder case.

How could any of this have happened? And now what?

The first thing I did was check the table drawer where I kept my passport, warranties, insurance papers, things like that. I put the phone down on top of all that and shut the drawer.

Seeing the passport provoked a wild thought. Taking it, leaving the country, taking up my life somewhere new as though nothing had happened. I traveled seldom, so it would seem suspicious. I had often thought of living elsewhere. Malta, perhaps. English was the official language in Malta. Maybe I should...

I stopped myself from following this train of thought. I realized that an odd kind of panic was taking over. Almost as if I were separate from myself, I stroked my upper arm and said, "Shhhh, shhh," out loud.

Once I was calmed, I realized because of Farley's age and the youth of the victim, there might eventually be newspaper and possibly television coverage from Austin. The most immediate place to look would be our local newspaper. I could learn all the details. It was all very sad. Farley would have to stand trial and the parents—Janice and whatever her husband's name was—would have to face Farley in court. Ray. That was his name.

. . .

But what about me? What about the phone I had? Could the phone be traced? Even if it was the dead boy's phone, what, if anything, could anyone learn from it? Why was I so convinced that it held information that was vital?

I had never owned a cell phone, had never wanted one. I had been amused by the absorption that people with cell phones exhibited. But I'd seen police shows on television and knew that most phones contained some sort of tracking device. I also knew that they contained a card that could be removed, rendering the phone dead and untraceable. But would removing it delete whatever was on the phone?

I opened the drawer and took the phone out again. I pressed the various buttons on it but nothing seemed to work. I wasn't sure how to proceed.

I would have to get a cell phone of my own and learn to use it. Otherwise, my possession of the victim's phone—if that was indeed what I had—would be for naught.

Although it seemed quite out of place in our little town, there was a huge and ugly electronics store in town, Electrix. I would go there in the morning and learn what I could about those gadgety phones.

I hesitated. I would be revealing myself to the salespeople at Electrix as way behind the times. Did I care? Was I the only person in Lost Pines with a landline only? A landline I use only if I have to, for business.

I felt foolish. I knew I'd have to stop myself from explaining to salespeople why I'd never needed a cell phone in the past. Of course, then they'd want to know why I wanted one now. I could make a story up, invent a son or daughter who insisted I have one. Something. Unless I steeled myself, and realized it was none of their business. None of their business. I felt myself harden. I would be immune to whatever attitude the salesforce at Electrix presented to me.

Did everyone go through machinations like this making decisions, or was I the only one in the world who did? A part of me that wanted to be warmer, be liked, meet friends for dinner or for lunch. But then, when I am around other people, that part shrinks away. I am typically bored, impatient. I would rather be in a room alone than with the person talking to me, talking at me. Right this minute, I am trying to think if there is anyone anywhere who might interest me and I can think of no one.

My home is where I am happy. When I travel, I am always relieved to be home. More than relieved. Just being with my things in a space that is all mine gives me solace, satisfaction. Sometimes I think of my life in kind of biblical terms: On the seventh day she rested and everything was exquisite. Something like that, odd as it may seem.

I believe my home kept me alive when I was waiting to die. I'd wake in a bedroom I adored and walk into a carefully curated bathroom. I sometimes reached out and touched objects that I loved, often remembering when and how I'd acquired them. I am not ashamed to say that, while most would say they love other people, if I were honest, I'd admit that I love things.

I don't mean to sound as though I'm bragging or self-centered, but I have a way of seeing and combining, a way of juxtaposing this and that so it all comes together just right.

Instead of feeling like the house had come together just right, I had felt that the home of Farley and Leona had walls and especially furnishings that would close in upon me and trap me there.

A sudden thought occurred: Perhaps the walk that Farley took each morning was his way of escaping the spell of the house he lived in, at least briefly.

CHAPTER FIVE

DECEMBER 23, 2019

The local newspaper came out twice a week. Tuesday and Saturday. I went to the convenience store nearest me and snatched a copy before they all disappeared. I went from front to back of the paper in minutes and saw nothing about the murder on the Riverwalk.

Instead, there were two whole pages of Letters to Santa, dumb letters from local children that the paper had solicited and printed. Two whole pages! The letters were repetitive and greedy, and I pictured Leona Clement reading them aloud to Farley, "Farley, Listen to this one! Isn't it precious?"

I told myself that once Christmas was over, which would be days from now, things would go back to normal and the newspaper would issue a full report of the crime. But now, right now, there was nothing.

I Googled "beating, Lost Pines," "murder, Lost Pines," "Farley Clement, Lost Pines." The latter yielded an old story about Farley's retirement. In addition to teaching, he had translated the work of an obscure German mathematician into English.

DECEMBER 25, 2019

On Christmas morning, I forced myself to go to the Riverwalk. It was not quite light, and all the holiday paraphernalia was lit up. Santa tipped his hat over and over again as I got out of my car in the parking lot.

Snoopy wagged his big white tail.

An overly metallic version of "Hark, the Herald Angels Sing" played in the background.

Someone seemed to be sitting on a bench at the picnic tables to the right. Someone in dark clothing. The figure stirred, stood, and came toward me.

I hurried away.

I don't know what I thought. I was a bit afraid, a bit annoyed.

"Hey," the figure said. "Hey, wait. It's me, Carl. Hey, wait."

I was relieved to learn that it was Carl. Perhaps that's why my hello was friendlier than it might have been.

But I stiffened when he said, "I been hoping to see you." He assessed me and grunted out a laugh.

I mustered a smile.

"I want to talk to you about the cellphone," Carl said.

I tensed again.

"You remember, don't you?"

I nodded. I felt my face flush.

"You were there when I handed it over to that cop, right?"

Oh, *that* phone. His phone. Not the phone I'd found. "Yes," I said. "I remember."

"Yeah, well the cops are saying they never got it. They're saying I ought to have some kind of receipt or something."

I thought I'd heard the policeman say he was going to give Carl a receipt. I mentioned this and Carl shook his head.

"The cop never came back, but I just figured it would be okay, you know."

I attempted to console him. "Maybe they still need the phone. Maybe they'll give it back when they finish with it."

"Yeah, well, they could take the video off of it and give the fu...," he stopped himself and bit his lower lip. "They could put it on their computer and give the phone back to me, you know."

"How exactly would they do that?" I said, genuinely interested.

Carl laughed, or maybe I should say 'scoffed.' "Phones don't just take pictures anymore. They take videos too. So I got Farley wailing on the kid."

Oh, Brave New World! "How would they put the video on their computer?"

"They could hook the phone to the computer. You know, with a cord. I forget the name of it. And then they wouldn't need my phone anymore," Carl said. "But listen, if they don't give it to me next time I ask, will you go there with me and tell them that you, you know, witnessed them taking it?"

"I would go, Carl, but I'm not sure it would help." In truth, it would probably hurt.

"Well, whatever," Carl said. "What's your name?"

"Eleanor Armitage," I said.

"Carl Sewicki. You live near here?" he probed.

"Not far," I allowed.

"Maybe you can, like, give me your phone number or your address or something," he said.

I squirmed, maybe not outwardly, but something inside me was saying 'No,' 'No,' 'No.' "Let's just plan on running into each other here," I said. "We almost always seem to."

"Yeah, okay. Thanks," he said. "You gonna walk?" He gestured toward the path ahead.

"No," I told him. "I'm running a little late."

He looked suspicious. And he was right to be, it was true. I just didn't want to walk with him, or anybody. And since he and I would be starting down the path together, walking with him right now would be unavoidable. "To tell you the truth," I forced a slight smile, "I don't know if I'm ready to go down there."

His face relaxed. "Oh, yeah. Yeah. I get it." With that he gestured toward the pathway—the place where Farley had beaten the boy. "You gotta do it, though. You know. Get over it."

"Maybe tomorrow," I told him.

"Well," he said, "Merry Christmas."

"Same to you," I said.

When I turned to walk away, I felt sadness. Sadness for myself. It was Christmas morning and there I was, alone, avoiding contact, not even willing to say, "Merry Christmas" out loud. *Same to you.* Was that the best I could muster?

There was no getting around it: I had to get the phone I'd found to work and see what was on it. At least I had to know whether it was the dead boy's phone. I resolved to go to the big electronics store, Electrix, and ask about it. Or maybe better yet, just buy a similar phone and learn how to work it.

The store was huge and open, even though it was Christmas morning. A sign, however, indicated they would close at noon. There were no customers and the table in front of the store where I'd seen young people selling cell phones was empty. I wandered up one aisle and down the other and it was just like the police station: seemingly deserted.

Anything you had to plug in seemed to be there: refrigerators, washers, dryers, televisions, even things for the car like radios and cd players. It was there in the car stereo section that, finally, I saw another human.

He turned to look at me. The logo on his shirt indicated that he worked at the store.

"Merry Christmas," he said.

"Thank you," I replied. "I want to buy a cell phone."

"Oh, today's not the day," he said. "You have to sign up for a service and those folks are out for the holiday." A certain amount of sarcasm crept into his voice as he said the last four words.

"Well, maybe you can tell me about the brand I'm interested in," I said.

"Sure enough," he said. "iPhone? Android? Or..."

I had taken the phone out of the case with the skull on it to examine it, so I knew what it was. "An iPhone," I told him. Although I had the phone I'd found in my pocket, I decided not to show it. If I already had a phone, why would I be buying one and asking how the thing works?

"That's what I've got, an iPhone," he said, taking the exact same phone out of his pocket. "This is the latest one."

"So how does it work?"

He looked at me as if I'd just fallen to earth from a distant star. "You've never had a cell phone?" he asked. His voice dripped with incredulity. He looked around the store, as if wishing he could share the information about me with another salesperson, but no such luck. I could picture him, "You won't believe this woman.," he'd say. "Came in Christmas Day and..."

He raised his eyebrows and sighed. "Well, okay. You turn it on," he said, showing me an almost invisible button to the right of the screen. Immediately a screen opened up displaying the time. "Then you look up here," He pointed to a little battery icon in the corner, "and this tells you how much juice it has."

"Okay," I said. "But what if it doesn't have, uh, juice?" I presumed he meant electricity.

"You charge it," he said. "The charger comes with it and you plug this in," he set a square thing up and then detached the wire from it. "This you can put directly into the computer."

"And then?"

He had that look again. The look that said I couldn't possibly be for real. "Then you either put your finger here or you tap in the password."

"Password." Oh, god, the password. Passwords were the reason I hated using my computer. I had to write down passwords for everything. Email, Amazon, eBay, you name it.

"You pretty much need to put a password in to get into the phone. That's the first thing you have to do. They can show you when you sign up," he said. Now he seemed eager to see me gone. My lack of knowledge was too much for him.

"Okay, assuming I put a password in and then I forget it," I tried.

"Then you use the finger i-d. It reads your fingerprint."

"So there's no way to get into the phone without either your finger or the password?"

"Probably not. You remember that terrorism thing out in California where the FBI wanted to get into the terrorists' phone and couldn't?"

"No."

"Well, they couldn't. I don't know if they ever did. It was out in San Bernadino, I think, couple of years ago. But I don't know. Maybe it was super encrypted or something, since the guys were terrorists."

"And then?"

"Then it's no way, Jose," he laughed. "But lady, I don't know what you'd do if it stopped reading your fingerprint and you didn't know what to tap in. It's one or the other."

"When will the cell phone people be back?"

"Tomorrow," he told me. "Tomorrow is, like, our busiest day. Lots of sales and stuff."

"Well, thank you," I told him. "But can you keep on showing me things about the phone? You know, so I don't look as dumb as I obviously am when I come back."

"Sure thing," he said, expansive now. And so I learned how to do a lot of things, all kinds of things, including taking pictures and videos and viewing them. I insisted on buying a charger even though that would come with the phone when I bought one tomorrow, if I did. That seemed to throw him for a bit of a loop. But that way, when I got home, I could fire the dead phone up and worry about what the password might be.

DECEMBER 26, 2019

I allowed the boy's phone to charge overnight, but there was still the password thing to overcome. I also wondered what I would do if someone called the boy. Should I answer? My hands trembled when I held the lighted phone in my hands. But try as I might, nothing I did unlocked it.

I tried searching "San Bernadino, cell phone, terrorists" and learned that, regarding the phone the salesman had talked about, Apple had been sued by the government for not opening it for them.

Well, the terrorist's phone, evidently, had been opened, and a spirited argument took place about whether or not the FBI had to tell Apple exactly how opening it had been done. Some people—the ones who posit 'alternative facts'—even wrote about how the phone had remained impenetrable, but that the FBI wanted Apple to think they'd opened it to drive them crazy.

What I read made me think I wouldn't be able to open the phone at all. But I still wanted to try the regular phone people at

Electrix, because that was all they did—talk to people about phones.

Meanwhile, I had concocted a new and I thought particularly clever lie. When I got to Electrix—unlike it had been Christmas morning, was now jammed to the gills with shoppers—I told the phone people that I'd bought the phone in a shop that had since gone out of business and that I wasn't able to open it because it was encrypted. I even added, "you know, like the San Bernadino terrorist's phone?" to my spiel.

"You sure you mean encrypted?" a young man with a tag that read Jessie asked. I blundered through an answer but it turned out that encryption wasn't the right word and that encryption was far more sophisticated and extensive than a password. The boy's phone was "password protected." I was told that nearly everyone's was.

"I can reset the password for you," Jessie said. "But I need your email address."

I was about to give it to him, when the guy standing next to him hollered. "Wait a minute, Jessie. If you do it that way, you'll clear everything off the phone." An argument between the two salespeople ensued and I decided not to try whatever method I was about to hear because I didn't want to risk losing whatever was on the phone. While the two men were still arguing, I slipped the phone back into my pocket and left the store.

I was on my own. I passed a bin where people turned in their old equipment for recycling purposes and resisted a brief urge to toss the phone in with the other things. I could go home, I could forget all of this ever happened, I could break free of this strange streak of curiosity that had swept me up and be done with it. I could recover my life.

But I didn't throw the phone away. I knew the phone was important. I don't know how I knew, but I did.

I am not technologically savvy, nor do I want to be. I use what technology I must in order to earn my living, but beyond that, nothing. I don't give any of my information out so that I'm not tormented by junk email or junk phone calls. My landline suits me.

I was willing to buy a cell phone to try to open the one I'd found, but only for that reason. I was relieved that I didn't have to. Of course, I still didn't know if I could be tracked the way criminals with cell phones were, but I decided to take my chances. Lost Pines' police force seemed to be too incompetent to do anything complicated. Or too uninterested. But what should my next step be?

CHAPTER SIX

DECEMBER 27, 2019

I went to the Riverwalk the next morning hoping to run into Carl. I don't even know why. I felt an odd sort of connection to him, maybe based on what we'd seen together. He was ticked off at the local police, too, another thing that made me trust him.

I walked from the parking lot to the place where the beating had taken place. It was just a turning around point, the place where the path ended. As nearly as I could figure, the spot was just beneath Farley and Leona's property.

Their home was wildly overgrown, especially when compared to the terraced property beside it. Farley and Leona—assuming they owned their property outright—sat on a prime piece of real estate. If they cleared the mess out back, they could call the property 'waterfront'!

I recalled their place from the front, when I'd returned their dog. The rear of the place was something I wouldn't even have suspected when I looked at the property from the street. The back could be deduced from the Riverwalk if I knew where to look.

A few times I'd made it a point to walk to the place where Farley and Leona had their gate.

The entire lot in back was steep and overgrown. Poison ivy seemed to have taken over. But there was a thick wooden staircase amid the jungle. It didn't look very old, and except for the overgrowth, it was perfectly serviceable. I couldn't really see it unless I was willing to push the brush away and brave the poison ivy. But there was an actual gate in the wrought iron fence surrounding all the places that bordered the Riverwalk. Something I vaguely recalled that the city had agreed to pay for when construction of the walkway was approved. That had been years ago, maybe the first year I'd moved to Lost Pines.

I wondered if Farley used this staircase. There was so much vegetation that I rather doubted that he did. I imagined what I'd have to do to take that route.

Well, I'd have to go home and change first. I'd have to cover my arms and legs completely and maybe wear a babushka to protect my face. I could go up those stairs and...what? I'd be in Farley's backyard. I'd either have to go back down or knock on Farley's back door and go through their house to the street. Or else get caught creeping along the side of their house. What would be the point? *Great idea, Eleanor,* I thought. Then I looked at the staircase again, wondering why I had envisioned myself climbing it at all.

CHAPTER SEVEN

The *Lost Pines Gazette* was housed in a storefront on Main Street. I had never been inside. I was surprised at how shabby it was, with vinyl linoleum missing huge patches and dirty walls that looked as though they were made of cardboard.

A voice in a room off to the left called out. "Help you?"

I went to the doorway and saw a teeny woman with a sort of Beatles' haircut. "Are you the editor?" I asked. Of course I knew she was. Lost Pines isn't a huge metropolis.

"Juanita Star. Yes, I am indeed." She eyed me up and down. I knew from the way she pursed her lips that she'd seen me before. I felt a stab of belligerence but ignored it.

I was still in the doorway to her office and could see a room with several desks beyond, but no one was working at any of them.

She seemed to know what I was thinking. "Holidays," she said. "Wanna sit?" She indicated a chair that faced her desk. "You are Miss Armitage, are you not?"

I sat down and leaned toward her, damned if I'd be put off. "Eleanor Armitage," I said. "I was on the Riverwalk the other day and I saw a man—Farley Clement, the science teacher—hitting a young man on the ground."

"Yes, I heard about it. Apparently, it was what the young man deserved. Are you wondering why we didn't cover it?"

"Well, yes."

Juanita Star sighed and shook her head. I knew she was thinking of all the times I'd written to persuade her to cover a story I'd had a personal stake in. Although I'd sent in letters and even attempted to write an article myself, she hadn't responded to my efforts. She hadn't answered me at all, which, to my mind, was an insult.

The silence was uncomfortable. As though she was deciding what she ought to do. We were alone in the office, she and I. Was she afraid? I hadn't been that much of a pest, had I? "Eleanor Armitage," she said at last.

She waved her hand as though surrendering and leaned toward me. "On this thing in the park, oh, look, hon. I just couldn't bear to do it. Put a thing like that in with all the Letters to Santa. I know that doesn't make me a big crusading editor like in the movies but imagine everybody reading that right at Christmas. I used my editorial judgment and held off."

She was smiling and I know she expected me to smile back, but I couldn't. Without meaning to, I blurted out, "Is that why you didn't cover the hit and run? Because it was Fourth of July?"

I don't know what possessed me to say that. I really hadn't wanted to.

She took a deep breath. "Oh my God," she said. "I don't have time for this."

When she said "this," I assume she meant the way I'd prodded her after Megan's death.

She held up a finger as in wait-a-minute and started looking for something on her computer. Then she said, "I'll print it off for you." She hit buttons on her computer and in the room beyond I heard a machine start up. She had to go into that room to get whatever she'd printed.

She handed a page to me. The type on it was written in a narrow column, just the way it would be in the newspaper. It said:

POTTS YOUTH LOSES LIFE

Lost Pines police reported that a Potts boy lost his life on the Lost Pines Riverwalk on Thursday. Brandon Sterling, age 14, died as a result of injuries incurred in a beating. Police said the beating was delivered by a Lost Pines citizen whose name has been withheld. Several witnesses as well as the police said that Sterling had attempted to rob or otherwise assault the citizen, who retaliated. Police say it is unlikely that any charges will be filed.

"So that's it?" I asked. I could feel my anger rising.

"It's no different from any of the crimes we write up."

Flat, devoid of color and emotion or any semblance of caring. I was filled with contempt. I could just imagine how she might have covered my best friend's death.

LOCAL ACTIVIST LOSES LIFE

Megan McCann died on Hwy 72 on fourth of July weekend. She was hit by a car, driver unknown and unsought.

. . .

I felt myself trembling.

She seemed to soften. "Did you know the boy?" she asked.

"No. But I was there. I saw what Farley Clement did to him." I know my face wrinkled at the thought.

"It's a good thing Farley had his wits about him," Juanita Star agreed. You can keep that page," she said, turning back to her computer screen. "Thanks for stopping by."

"Thank you," I said mechanically. I folded the article and slipped it into my pocket.

After this encounter, I sat in my car for a while, wondering at how sad I felt. I tried to figure out why but couldn't. Maybe it was because this monumentally large event had been reduced to a few bland words? But also, maybe it was because my friend's death hadn't been put into words at all. What kind of newspaper was this?

I became aware of something, a change in the light. It was Juanita Star, practically on her knees beside my low-slung car. I powered the window down. She made only brief eye contact with me when she spoke. "Here's the police report," she said, jamming it toward me. "It's got a little more in it." Without waiting, she stood up and made her way back to her office.

I had thought of her as a cold person, but the fact that she'd come outside to give me the report made me feel that maybe she did have a heart after all.

The police report was no better than the article had been, except that it contained the address of Janice and Ray Sterling in Potts and said they had been in town looking at houses because they were planning to move to Lost Pines. At their son's request, they had dropped him at the Riverwalk and had planned to pick him up when they'd finished looking at property.

Potts. I didn't know anything about it except that it was about 40 miles away. I'd seen a road sign or two. I wondered about the boy's parents. Would they still want to move to Lost Pines, where their child had died? I rather doubted it.

I went home and sat at my computer. I Googled Potts and found out that, compared to Lost Pines, it was tiny, about a quarter of the size. People were probably more petty there than they were here, especially since Austin was so close to us. A lot of the people in Lost Pines worked in Austin, so we probably qualified as a bedroom community to the big city.

We had pretty much everything here. The supermarket had a huge selection of expensive cheeses and wine galore and even an olive bar with a great antipasto selection. Potts, on the other hand, was probably the boonies.

But even there, people had cell phones. Cell phones were everywhere.

I ended up Googling iPhones and was amazed at the variety of colors that were available. If I ever were to get one, I decided, it would be rose gold, a kind of copper-tinged golden tone, very pretty. And I wouldn't buy a case, I decided. Why would anyone do that?

I opened the drawer where I'd put the boy's case. It was thin, good leather, maybe from Italy. It was stitched rather than glued. I folded the flap of it over and that was when I saw that someone had inked something inside the case. I turned it inside out and examined it under my desk lamp.

It said *nopussy4U*, written with a silver sharpie. Given the scatological nature of the inscription, I had no doubt that this phone belonged to Brandon Sterling, the victim.

It made me blush. But there it was: the password. I had no

doubt about it, even though I was loathe to put my fingers on the keys to type it in.

With that, I began to scroll through various texts and emails and photos. Yes, this was definitely the kid's phone.

Messages were all but incomprehensible with various abbreviations and phonetically spelled words. Photos were odd. There was one of a dead dog lying by the side of a road, dried blood around his head and his body swollen as if he'd been there for a long time. There was also the picture of a dead rabbit with an avulsed eyeball. The photo was so crisp that I could see the flies on the rabbit's head.

Did that mean that Brandon Sterling was a psychopath?

I shook the thought away. These were animals he'd come across, not animals he'd killed.

I moved on from the still pictures to the video section. I saw a young girl lying naked on a bed and heard a voice—Brandon's?—telling her to lean back and spread her legs. She whined that she wouldn't, not in front of the camera, and the video ended there.

Then there was a frozen visual of Janice and the sound of her saying, "Why can't you be more like Alex?" and the boy, presumably Brandon, mouthing in falsetto, "Why why why why why?"

Next was a fragment of television news which revealed that the son of the man who had been in the President's own cabinet had attacked his mother with a baseball bat and had fractured her skull. Then Brandon's comment before the video went black, "Way to go!"

The next one was a selfie, Brandon holding the camera at arm's length. "This is Lost Pines, the lame little town that Janice and Ray want me to grow up in. No shit. Janice says I need a change of scenery, a fresh start. Sound familiar? She's been saying this crap for the last hundred years."

Behind Brandon was a patch of thick greenery. Was it the Riverwalk? Was it, perhaps the spot where the boy had been killed?

The first salesperson I'd encountered at Electrix on Christmas Day had shown me something about enlarging the pictures. He'd done it with his fingers, kind of pinching the screen and pulling a section of the photo closer that way.

I tried it on a corner of this photo and yes, that part of the picture grew larger. I moved to another section and zoomed up on a healthy stand of poison ivy. And yes, I could see some of the railing of the staircase in Farley's back yard!

I enlarged another section and could see the black wrought iron fence. It was clearly the back of Farley's property.

I managed to get the photo back to its original state and watched it as a video from the beginning. Yes, the boy's angry soliloquy.

"Yes," the boy went on. "Janice thinks she can bring me here and I can start in a new school with a clean slate." He laughed, or rather, cackled.

Behind him, in the upper left hand corner of the screen, I saw a smear of gray. The gray grew larger as the video went on. The gray approached young Brandon from behind and Brandon was unaware of it.

"Clean slate. What the fuck does that mean, anyway? Was my slate dirty? If I knew what a slate was, I would tell you."

The gray seemed very close now. A shape began to emerge. The image was quite blurry, but unmistakably became a person.

At that point, the boy turned around and held the phone in front of him. "What do you want, old man?" the kid shouted, the camera wobbled on Brandon's shoes. Then the camera was raised and briefly there was Farley. Farley, wearing the twisted face that I had seen in person that dreadful day. Farley with his arms raised above his head.

The boy turned and tried to run and video on the phone became jumbled until the phone finally rested on a plot of ground. The sound, however, was crystal clear. The sound of Farley's cane against the boy's head. The sound of splintering and then, quite quickly, of mush.

I was sickened. I rushed to the bathroom and vomited into the toilet. My hands shook. Clearly, I had to get this video to the authorities, but who? I could not imagine going back to the Lost Pines police. They already had their story and certainly I wouldn't be able to convince them. I rather doubted I could even persuade them to watch what I'd unearthed. And anyway, I didn't want to give them the satisfaction of solving the case, even if they did listen to what I had to say.

"Hey, it's me, and I've got proof here that..." One of your finest citizens, a man you think was defending himself, is a stone cold killer. That would go over big. They'd probably destroy the evidence rather than admit they were wrong.

I had a reputation in Lost Pines. I don't know where it began and I certainly didn't feel it was deserved, but for some unknown reason, I'd been marked as someone who was, well, possibly quite crazy. It had to do with a man in town that had swindled Megan, my only friend. Actually, he'd swindled the government too and I'd tried to bring it to the government's notice, but was turned away. I wrote to the District Attorney and he told me to go to the police, that he prosecuted cases after the police brought charges. The police were the worst; they sent me away. I wrote to both of my senators and got form letters back from one of them thanking me for my interest. And meanwhile, the swindler got voted onto the Lost Pines city council.

I never stopped thinking about it, even though my friend was long dead.

After she died, it was like I inherited her obsession. I pushed harder. I even wrote to the IRS, but learned that no one cared. But everything I did, every time I accused the man, people seemed to treat me more and more like a leper until finally I took my leprosy and locked myself away.

I didn't need to see anybody. Screw them all. And then the doctor made me walk on the goddam Riverwalk.

All of a sudden, what I needed to do shone before me like some Old Testament revelation. The parents. The boy's parents. They would want to know their son was innocent. They would do something, surely. I could give them the phone, then stay out of it and let them seek the justice they deserved.

CHAPTER EIGHT

DECEMBER 27, 2019

It was still fairly early, so I got into my car and headed south. I drove around Potts, which seemed a nice enough little town. The houses were modest but well-kept. Nearly all of them were still decorated for Christmas, but, because it was daylight, the Santas and the sleighs and the reindeer, even the stables with Baby Jesus inside, looked shopworn, even tawdry. I was armed with Janice and Ray Sterling's address, but I didn't know the town, didn't know the streets, so I tried to drive a grid, a sort of pattern that would take me past all the streets until one registered as theirs.

Well, of course, what I was doing looked suspicious and soon enough a police car behind me signaled me to pull over.

I watched the officer approach my side mirror, and I found myself thinking of Sandra Bland, the black woman who was pulled over and hauled off to jail where she killed herself. Or they killed her.

But this officer was smiling. I pressed the button that lowered the window and he asked, "Are you lost, ma'am?"

Just then a scent overtook me. It was the citrus-y smell of 4711, a hand soap my parents had used. I was lost in the memory for a second, but then the officer reminded me. "Ma'am?"

"Yes," I said. "I'm looking for Grimes Road." Hadn't 4711 been discontinued years ago? I remembered reading that or hearing that or something.

"Did you hear me, ma'am?" the officer asked.

"Would you tell me again, please?"

He cocked his head. I think he was thinking of telling me to get out of the car. So I confessed. "It's your hands. That smell. My mother and father used it."

"Good old 4711," he agreed. And he seemed to relax when he said it. "So, you want Grimes, right? That would be out of town a-ways," he said. "I can point you in the right direction if you want, but you still have to go, oh, I don't know, couple of miles."

"Thanks," I said, and waited for instructions.

"There's just three houses out on Grimes. Who you looking for?"

"Janice Sterling. We went to school together and I was near the town and thought..."

"You know what's happened to the Sterlings?" he interrupted.

"No, what?"

"They just lost a son."

"Oh, no!" I feigned shock. "Sounds like she'll need a friend."

"I don't know," he said. "It's all really fresh. They might be out making arrangements as we speak. It was their boy, Brandon."

"Brandon," I repeated.

"Can't say he wasn't asking for it," the officer went on. "Tried to rob some guy up in Lost Pines and turned out the guy whomped him dead. Talk about justice."

"Where's Lost Pines?" I asked.

"Forty miles north of here," the officer said. "Some people said they—the Sterlings—were moving there to give Brandon a fresh start, him starting high school and all. Some fresh start."

"Was Janice having trouble with Brandon?" I asked, all innocence. "She didn't tell me anything about it."

"Nothing but trouble. Marijuana, beer, you name it. Hotwired a car and took it for a joy ride. And that was just for starters. Everybody in town knew to look out for Brandon Sterling. Stands to reason they'd want to move out of Potts."

"I think I'd better get back on the road. How do I get to Grimes?"

"I'll lead you out to where the road starts. Then you can be on your own. But I'll need to see your license and insurance to make out a service call. To account for my time."

A cold chill ran through me. Now, not only would there be an official record of my being here in town, but the officer would see that I actually lived in Lost Pines, even though I'd asked where it was a few moments ago.

I reached for my purse and made a show of looking through it. "Comb," I said, taking it out and putting it on the passenger seat. "Address book," placing that atop the comb. Then I rustled through a bunch of papers in an exaggerated way. "Oh, here's that shopping list! I'll be darn." I pretended to read it.

"Okay, okay," the officer said. "You head out the street you're on and when you come to Whitworth, you turn right and just keep on going. Grimes will be on your right once you're out a-ways. You'll know it's coming up because there's a rest stop right there at the turn."

"Thank you so much," I said, remembering to smile. I read his nametag. "Really, thank you, Officer Randall."

"Glad to be of help." He reached towards the brim of his hat as though about to tip it.

Ordinarily I would have roared away. I love the pickup that my little Mercedes has. But instead, I pulled sedately onto the street. I even used my turn signal when I pulled out.

The Sterling house was obvious. There were, as the officer had said, just three houses along the road. But the Sterling house seemed dead, unoccupied. There were no vehicles that I could see, although there was a roofed shed beside the house that could have housed maybe three separate cars.

Maybe as Officer Randall had said, Janice and Ray Sterling were making funeral arrangements.

It was an opportunity to look inside the house. Inspecting the way they lived would tell me something about them, something more than what I already knew. It's unfair of me, I know, but I tend to judge people by the things they surround themselves with. A house and the things in it speak plenty.

The Sterling house itself was beautiful, a Craftsman made of dark brick. It had a substantial wraparound porch, brick and concrete and at least ten feet wide. It was a shame, I thought, that they'd allowed that low-end metal shed to have been erected so close to the home.

I drove up the driveway and parked. Then I thought better of it and backed out onto Grimes Road. Had the Sterlings seen my car? I tried to remember. Well, I already had a story prepared for the occasion. I knew they were grieving and I was stopping by in case they needed any help back in Lost Pines.

In my little fantasy, I would hand them the phone and ask innocently, could it possibly belong to their son? With every step I took, however, I became more and more cowardly. What would I do? I had to get the phone to them, but some other way. By the time I'd reached the steps to the front porch, I decided I'd leave the phone somewhere near the house as though they'd missed seeing it earlier.

Yes, they'd be puzzled, but in all their grief, maybe they would just take it and be satisfied.

I walked up the wide concrete stairs and went to the front window. It seemed quite comfortable inside. Mission furniture. A decorated but unlit Christmas tree. A pile of untouched, still-wrapped presents.

I moved on to another window, the dining room. Seating for eight. Instead of plates on the table, I saw ribbons and bows and rolls of gay wrapping paper. Scissors, tape.

The kitchen, quite modern, unexpectedly so. The refrigerator door, however, was open. When it closed, I saw him and stifled a scream. It was the dead boy, the one whose picture I'd seen. The Before picture. But it couldn't be, because I'd also seen the blood-drenched, pulpy mess that was After.

I froze momentarily and so did the boy. When he moved, I was able to move as well. I felt my heart pump and my head going hot.

I turned away, stumbled, recovered and ran back to my car. I heard the front door of the Sterling house open and a young voice shout, "Hey!" The dead boy. The dead boy had seen me and was calling out to me.

I didn't turn. I jumped into the car and turned so hastily that I almost lodged the rear end of the car into a bar ditch. Then I roared away, roared all the way back to the road to Potts, planning to intersect with the highway back to home. I felt dizzy, clammy, cold but sweat-drenched. I had seen a dead person. I was entitled to fear.

Back in Potts proper, I heard the siren and saw the flashing lights in my mirror. Once again, I pulled over. I saw the very same officer as before walking resolutely toward my little car. I rolled the window down. "I'm sorry," I said, trying to sound halfway calm. "Janice and Ray weren't there and I..."

"You what?" He used my pause to prod me.

"I saw..." When words failed me, I reached out the window and grabbed Officer Randall's forearm. Very unlike me. And my seeming inability to speak, that was unlike me too.

"You saw Alex, and it freaked you right out."

Alex?

"I saw Brandon."

"Just be glad it wasn't Brandon you saw," the officer said. "By the way, this time, I'm gonna ask you again for your license and all and I want to see them. Because you went through that stop sign back there without even slowing down."

"I was terrified," I said.

He looked at me for a long time. Then he said, "Listen. Go up and turn left on Rochester. Two blocks and you'll see a little store called Sunshine. They got a couple tables in the back. I think you and me should maybe have a cup of coffee or a root beer and do a little talking."

"You drive slow now. And mind you, you'll have to stop at Rochester at the sign. Make sure you do, 'cause I'll be right in the back of you."

Yessir. Root beer. Would that count as a date in a town as backward as Potts? Probably.

I waited outside the store and watched him getting out of his cruiser. He looked fit, but I supposed policemen had to keep themselves up. When he walked toward me, he seemed boyish, although I could tell he was approximately my age. He obviously hadn't moved up through the ranks of his police force. I wondered if his superior was younger than he was.

He stood in front of me, maybe six inches taller than I was, and he took his hat off. His hair was either gray or pale blonde, close-cropped; again, I assumed, a police thing. It meant he didn't have a band of smashed hair, however. A smile seemed to come to his face quite often and quite naturally. If I were talking to someone about him, I'd have described him as fairly cute.

But there was more, probably attributable to his uniform, his job. I felt a sense of safety in his proximity. By driving to Potts, indeed, by my heightened curiosity about the boy's murder, I had ventured out of what people might call my "comfort zone."

So right there, in the Sunshine General Store, at a card table back beside the cold drink refrigerator doors, I promised Officer Randall that I would tell him all, though I didn't intend to. Not everything. I did give him my driver's license, which meant he would know I'd lied about Lost Pines.

He left the license on the table in front of him and kept looking from me, my face, to the photo on the license. It was as though he thought the license had been forged by some mob connection.

"Everything you told me is a lie," Officer Randall said. "All of it."

I hung my head. Tears welled up in my eyes and, like it or not, spilled over. I was wearing a long-sleeved shirt, so I mopped my face with my right cuff.

"You don't know Janice or Ray Sterling at all," he concluded. He crossed his arms and stared at me. My turn.

"I've met them," I said.

"Uh-huh." He leaned back in his chair, arms still crossed.

I tried to think of what that might mean in terms of body language. "I was there. I saw the boy's body. There's no way that boy could have survived."

Officer Randall rocked forward and uncrossed his arms. He leaned over the table toward me. "I really ought to let you stew, but I'm a pretty nice guy. The Brandon boy didn't survive. He—Brandon—had a twin. Alex Sterling. Brandon was the evil twin and Alex was the good one. Just like in every dumbass horror movie you ever saw."

His voice was harsh. Why was this police officer so mad at me? I didn't deserve it. I was tired and scared and that was when I started crying in earnest. Huge sobs, loud ones. Gasps. This wasn't like me. I think it was the weight of everything that had gone on suddenly coming down on me.

Officer Randall grabbed a batch of napkins from a container on the table and handed them across to me. "Quit that," he whispered. "People are gonna think we're breaking up or something."

I realized the absurdity of this. Though I was sniffling and then, suddenly laughing, I eked out, "You'd break up with a girl on a root beer date?"

Then he started laughing too. We were both laughing like fools. We sort of got it together but then, when I honked loudly into the napkins when blowing my nose, we started up again. "Now," I said, "everyone will think we made up." My nose felt fizzy, but otherwise, I felt lighter than I had in quite a while.

"Oh, me." Officer Randall said, when we both more or less got control of ourselves. "Now, where were we?" He didn't sound mad anymore.

"Twins," I reminded him. "An evil twin and a good twin." It sounded insipid even as I said it.

"Yeah, well first, let me get this off my chest. It's unisex, this 4711 stuff. It was invented in 1792 by a Carthusian monk and was meant to be a medicine. Couple of years ago, the company was going to stop making it, but then they changed their mind. At first it was just a cologne, but now they have soap, too. I don't wear the cologne. I just buy the soap."

He had me laughing again.

"See?" he said. "Even down here in Potts, we have the Internet." He had obviously looked this up after our first encounter. I had to admit that it struck me as sweet.

Now, he had what I can only describe as a tease in his eyes, as if he knew what I was thinking. But then he grew serious. "Like I said, the Sterlings were looking to buy a place in Lost Pines so Brandon and Alex could start over again. Well, so Brandon could.

Because everyone here in Potts knows about how bad Brandon is. Was."

"How did you hear about the murder?" I asked him.

"Oh, it was a big deal. Lost Pines sent us a video of the whole thing."

It was from Carl Sewicki's phone, I knew. Which meant it wasn't the whole thing. The whole thing was the video that I had. The one I planned to give to Ray and Janice Sterling. The video I really ought to mention to Officer Randall, sitting across from me in the soda pop section of a little store in Potts.

"That old guy was banging on Brandon Sterling to beat the band. It was awful to watch."

"I know the video. I was there when Carl recorded it. I saw what the camera was seeing."

"Up close and personal," he said. "Must have been rough."

"Yes." If I were to tell him about finding the phone, about the footage that I had, now would be the time. But what would he say? He'd probably make me come to the police station and fill out a dozen forms and god knows what else.

I suddenly felt exhausted. I didn't think I could even stand up. Plus, from what Officer Randall had told me, Brandon's death seemed to solve a lot of problems for everyone. For all I knew, Janice and Ray were glad they didn't have bad boy Brandon to deal with anymore and their lives in Potts could just go on with Alex, the good son. And Farley wouldn't have to go to jail, leaving Leona alone.

A very good murder, all around. If this had been a *Law & Order* episode, the credit would begin to roll.

Officer Randall's voice startled me. "This Carl fellow. Is he your boyfriend?"

"Carl?" I laughed, conjuring up the burly image of Carl in his camo fatigues, pot belly and all. "No!"

"That bad, huh?"

"That bad." I began collecting my belongings, strewn across the table. I put them back into my bag. "Well, Merry Christmas, Officer Randall," I said, finding that I could indeed stand. The opportunity to tell him about the video had passed.

"Name is Connor," he said. "And the same to you." He cocked his head. That little tease came back into his eyes, "Eleanor?"

I looked at him with wonder. He'd put us on a first name basis, and it had happened so easily. If he'd been any other man, I'd have come down on him like a guillotine, but instead, I heard myself say, "Eleanor it is."

We shook hands. Characters in a Victorian parlor. But all the way down the highway, I adhered to the posted speed limit and smiled, thinking about the encounter.

I was still smiling when I arrived back in Lost Pines.

CHAPTER NINE

DECEMBER 28, 2019

The next morning, as soon as it was light enough, I drove to the Riverwalk and went quickly to the trail's end, the spot where the boy had died. Nothing marked that it had been a crime scene. No chalk outline of Brandon Sterling's body, no yellow crime tape.

I took my camera with me, wanting to photograph the place, including the fence and the staircase that led to Farley's. I shot the death site first. There was no sign of the blood and tissue that I'd originally seen there. Although there was no reason to expect that it hadn't been cleaned—if not by a city or police crew, by the flies and fire ants that stayed out year round.

I moved on toward Farley's fence. *Click, click, click.*

I think I was taking the photographs to show to Officer Randall. I corrected myself. To Connor, if ever I should encounter him again. In fact, it might be a good idea to contact him and offer the photos.

I had no romantic interest in him, but he didn't treat me like the Lost Pines crazy. He didn't seem to think I was crazy at all. I thought of him as an ally, and if anyone needed one after picking up that phone and watching that video, it was me.

I heard a rustling sound near the death site. A stand of bamboo was to the left of it, between the site and the riverbank. The noise had come from there. I wasn't afraid until the bamboo shook and Farley Clement, hands wrapped with bandages, stood up.

That was when I gasped.

"It's all right, dear. I won't bite," he said, and smiled. "I was just looking for something."

Right. Like maybe the cell phone belonging to the boy you beat to death. Of course I did not say that. I looked at Farley's hands. How, had he found it, would he have picked the phone up?

I should have bolted when I first saw him, but instead, as he approached me, I stepped closer to the wrought iron fence. Now he was in a spot where he could block any chance of escape on my part.

But what could he do with those bandages? They were thick, so that they looked a little like boxing gloves.

He didn't seem to recall that I had been at the murder, and given the state he'd been in, I wasn't surprised. He raised his hands up as if in surrender and laughed slightly. "Broken fingers, both hands, worst luck."

Ha ha ha.

I don't know what is wrong with me, because, instead of pushing past him toward home, I said, "What are you looking for? Maybe I can help."

He stared at me for a long time and I stared back. His mouth opened into a little O. He cocked his head to one side. He said, "You have it. You have the phone."

I do tend to blush, but now I felt a hot rush of blood through my veins and into my head. My face must have looked like a red balloon. But also, I was rooted to the spot. My legs felt like lead and I knew I couldn't even walk, much less run.

"I have the phone," I said, "...and I watched the footage. I saw what really happened."

There.

I went on. I don't know why. I just couldn't stop myself. I sounded angry, and I think I might have been. "You sneaked up behind him. He didn't know you were there. You stalked him the way a wild animal would stalk his prey."

Farley shook his head, no. "He ransacked the drawers in our kitchen. He took anything sharp that he could find. He pressed his fingers against the edges to make sure they were sharp enough."

What was he talking about? It was as though each of the two of us were talking to other people. I pressed on. "You raised the cane and your face was twisted in hatred. You beat him and beat him and beat him to death."

Farley looked up at the sky. His voice was anguished. "Leona had fallen. The tree was down. She was lying on the floor beside it. He was going to cut her. He was going to cause her pain. He was going to torture her." He dropped to his knees in front of me. "I had to. I had to." He raised his head and his eyes stared into mine. "He was going to kill my wife."

Those words seemed to undo him. He crumpled into a little ball right there on the walkway. His shoulders were shaking as he cried. I didn't know what to do. I thought about running, I tried to tell myself to run, but I couldn't. Worse, part of me felt that I had caused his collapse.

I stooped down and touched his shoulder. "Farley," I said. "Please get up."

He unfolded and straightened up, but was still on his knees. His nose was running and his cheeks were wet. "I always thought it was a gift. It was a gift until I saw that boy."

Maybe he was crazy. Yes, he had to be crazy. I was in the park, alone with him, standing near a spot where he'd murdered someone.

As though he'd read my mind, he said, "It was not murder. And he was not just 'someone.' He was someone bent on doing harm to Leona. He was going to murder my wife."

He was getting angry. I certainly didn't want that. I had to appease him somehow and, above all, I had to get away.

He was still on his knees and he was still looking into my eyes. He gestured toward the path that led back to where I'd parked my car. "Go," he said. "You can go. I never meant to keep you. I just wanted to talk." He put his hands on the ground and levered himself upright.

I got up as well, and not very gracefully. I dusted at my clothing.

While my head was down, he said, "Go on, Button. Run along."

Had I heard him correctly? Had he said what I thought I'd heard? Had he called me Button, the way my parents once did? And "Run along." How often my father had said that after he'd fixed something for me or solved some problem!

Farley dropped his gaze and stared downward. He was like a penitent child. It was as if he felt embarrassment for having reached into my past.

"Farley," I all but whispered.

Something in my voice emboldened him. He stared right at me again. "You kept the buttons in jelly glasses. You had a lot of blue ones. You had a lot of white ones. You needed more red ones and purple ones and you asked your mother if you could buy them."

He and I began to move in unison. We were heading toward a bench. The bench where I'd first met him. Our steps mirrored each other's, as if choreographed.

The two of us sat.

"You found very special buttons at a rummage sale. Buttons that looked like daisies," he smiled at me." They were untouched, still attached to the card."

As he spoke, I could see the daisy buttons exactly as I'd found them. There were six of them, as he said, they were still attached the way buttons in the store offered them for sale, anchored onto a thick white card.

I could not believe the things he knew. These were episodes I'd long forgotten, but when he mentioned them, I remembered.

"I have to stop," he told me. "When it just happens, it doesn't exhaust me, but when I have to concentrate and reach, it's exhausting." He leaned back on the bench and closed his eyes.

"Are you saying you are clairvoyant?" I asked.

He spoke without opening his eyes. "Yes. Some call it Second Sight."

Or Sixth Sense. "And you killed the boy because you had a vision of the boy hurting Leona?"

"Yes. It used to happen every now and then with my students. I would have a feeling, a faraway feeling of some kind, and then I would see them as adults. One would be a lawyer. Another a ballerina. Not all children, mind you."

"Certain children," I said.

"Yes. Certain children." He opened his eyes and pulled his head upright. He looked at me. "It was entertaining. I would tell Leona and she would laugh and we would both peruse the newspapers for word of children whom I'd taught. When we found one—when what I'd envisioned had come true—Leona would look at me with such admiration. Pure admiration. I felt gifted to be admired that way."

And then he'd seen Brandon and a vision that was vile.

I can't say I was an unbeliever. One of my favorite television shows a few years back was called *Medium*, about a housewife named Allison DuBois who could see into the future or the past. Her dreams frequently took her there. I remember when it first came on, there was a lot of publicity about a real psychic by that name. At least real enough to have worked with law enforcement helping to solve crimes.

But the biggest thing was something that happened to me at a pajama party where we all tried to coax forth our psychic gifts. There were about twelve girls at the party and we paired up. One girl was supposed to think really hard about a boy she liked and the other girl was supposed to describe him.

I really tried hard to concentrate, and I was irritated when I could overhear the other girls in the room saying things like, "He has an average build, and he likes football and..." They sounded stupidly vague to me. Meanwhile, I was concentrating, concentrating, and I did clearly see a suntanned boy walking away from me on a beach. One of his shoulders was higher than the other. I told the girl with whom I was partnered and she gasped and grabbed my wrist. She didn't say anything, but I knew from her reaction that I'd connected with something real. It turned out her boyfriend was a lifeguard and, because of a wrestling accident, his shoulders were mismatched.

The girl and I didn't go beyond this because it was just a party game and we were moving on to some other activity, but I've never forgotten her response, so different from the other girls who were squealing, "Oh, that's uncanny," "Oh, that's exactly right" to the generic descriptions they heard. Mine was specific. And I hadn't invented what I saw.

There was another incident not so long ago. I had the flu and had doped myself up with Nyquil in the middle of the day. Not the daytime Nyquil but the heavy duty stuff. I got up to go to the bathroom and I saw what looked like a drop of fresh blood on the bathroom floor.

I thought I'd cut myself, and examined my bare feet, but no. I wiped the blood up with some toilet paper and flushed the paper down the commode, puzzled, but too bleary to much care.

Later that day was when I learned that my good friend Megan

had been killed by a hit and run driver that afternoon. I went back to look at the spot on the bathroom floor, but of course I'd cleaned it up and there was nothing to indicate that the blood had really been there.

There was even a third incident. It happened when I was in college. I'd rented a room in the basement of a house, and a couple lived above me. I could hear the man accusing the woman of all sorts of dumb things and I could hear him slapping her. Once she came to my apartment and I took her in, let her sleep on the sofa.

The day after that incident, I was just out of the shower, naked. There was a window in the bathroom next to the driveway. I heard him pull in and stumble out of his truck, muttering obscenities. And suddenly, I knew, *knew*, he was coming to my apartment.

I grabbed my dirty clothes out of the hamper and quickly pulled them on. I made my way to the door and, when he pushed it open, there I was. I told him to get out. I told him I had already called police. He stopped dead and turned around and went to his own place.

If he'd pushed in and found me naked, I'm sure he would have beaten me the way he regularly beat his wife.

But what strikes me, looking back, is the certainty I'd had about his coming to my apartment. It was absolute knowledge and it saved me.

So when I asked Farley if he was clairvoyant, it was with respect rather than disbelief. I believed that sometimes the unbelievable does occur, even though believing that would add to my reputation as a kook.

I never talked about either of these incidents, but I think that's why I didn't scoff when I sat in front of the television watching Patricia Arquette playing Allison DuBois, the psychic. And that, too, is why I was willing to believe Farley.

. . .

We sat there in silence for a while and then he said, "Will you come home with me?"

"I..." I tried to remember the brutality I'd witnessed at his hands. I tried to think of an excuse, but nothing came to mind. I had no fear, not anymore.

Farley opened the wrought iron gate and it creaked appropriately. I was pliant, standing and walking to his side. Then he led me up the wooden stairs. They were surrounded by foliage but nothing was on them to block the way. It was mostly poison ivy, big shiny, healthy leaves. It hadn't been cold enough for it to die off.

Halfway up I had to call Farley to stop. I was winded, I told him and needed to catch my breath.

"You needn't be afraid," Farley said.

"I'm not afraid," I insisted. "I'm out of breath."

"Oh, the stairs, Yes, I suppose I get plenty of exercise by using those stairs. I should add that I still manage an occasional session at the school gym," he boasted.

That explained the uncanny strength he seemed to have when he was pounding on poor Brandon.

"Ready?" he asked, and, when I nodded, we continued the climb.

I remembered staring at these steps from the Riverwalk and imagining myself climbing them. Had that been a premonition?

Inside the Clement house it was Christmas all over again. The tree was all lit up and a big plate filled with gingerbread men was on the table.

Farley saw me looking at them. "Take one. They're Leona's specialty."

So I took one and bit its head off. Marveling, really at my own bravado.

"Let's sit down," Farley said.

"Where is Leona?" I asked.

"At the Pet Emporium," he said. "She took Sadie to the groomer. I would rather she not know why that boy had to die."

When Farley said that, I suddenly became aware of the stillness in the house. We were alone, Farley and I. Why had I come to the house with him?

But Farley was in no way threatening. "Please," Farley said. "Please would you either give me the phone or destroy it." There was no question mark at the end of what he said.

"I don't know..." I said.

"Miss Armitage, please don't make me embarrass you. I know far more than you would want me to know. I want that phone and I must have it. Surely you realize its importance. I simply cannot give you control."

What did he mean? What more could he know? And the odd way he was speaking. As though the words were coming through to him from the cosmos.

He leaned toward me. And changed! His face contorted. He was about to say something when I panicked.

I stood up. "Stop!" I shouted. I looked around the room and moved toward the hallway that led to the front door. I was not thinking straight.

Farley moved quickly and stood between the doorway and me. "I'm not trying to hurt you. I'm trying to show you that what I did to that boy was self-defense, though not in the way everyone assumed. I cannot let you keep that boy's phone."

"I don't have it with me," I said.

He smiled and his voice tightened. "What's wrong with you? What's wrong with you?"

That was when my body started to shake. "Please," I begged Farley. "Please don't."

I was sixteen when that episode took place. I'd gone on a date with a boy, Louis Figulski. We had gone to the movies and afterward, I'd let him take me to his home.

Peter Gabriel's *Sledgehammer* had just come out and he put it on really loud and fixed it so the song would keep repeating. That's when I figured his parents weren't home.

We made out, and I must say, I enjoyed it, enjoyed the way he touched me and kissed me. We began removing our clothing. I was avant garde even then. Like the heroine in *Flashdance*, I wore an oversized tee shirt I'd strategically ripped. It was still awkward, what with the tights I wore and underneath those, my panties. Still, he and I together managed to dispense with those impediments.

I leaned back on the sofa where we sat and he entered me fast and hard and started pounding me in rhythm to the song. My vagina was wet and slick and his penis didn't hurt. I had wanted this. I had wanted him. But now, as he began to pump inside me faster and faster, I felt I had, for him, ceased to exist.

I know now his intention was to come—to have an orgasm inside me—but for some reason, he couldn't. He grew crazed. Still pumping, he pulled his upper body away from mine and he began slapping me across the face. With each slap, he screamed, "What's wrong with you? What's wrong with you?" until very suddenly, he yanked himself away and stood up.

He didn't look at me but started putting himself back together. Pulling up his undershorts, his trousers, picking up his belt where he'd tossed it. When he held the belt, something in his expression changed.

For a long moment, I thought he was going to use the belt to strike me. I even thought I might die. I laid there, trembling, tears coursing down my cheeks, snot streaming from my nose.

Was he just going to stay there, staring at me? It seemed as though he would, but no. Finally, he went into another room.

Alone, I started putting my clothes back on. My ears were ringing. My cheeks stung from his slaps. Then, fully dressed, I sat on the sofa and waited.

Louis came back in and spoke without making eye contact with me. "No one will ever want you," he said. "Your cunt is a mile wide. It's a fucking bowling alley, too big."

Something was wrong with me. Something was wrong with my vagina. "Come on," he said. "I'll take you home."

The ride from his house to mine seemed to take forever. I didn't know what time it was, but I hoped my parents wouldn't be up to ask me how the date had gone. It was my first date. My only date. Ever.

I don't think Louis told anyone. I certainly never did. I surprised myself in the morning when my mom asked if I'd enjoyed myself. I'd laughed. "Bor-ing," I told her, rolling my eyes. Then she and I laughed. And that was that. From that moment on, I lived that lie.

Now, I looked over at Farley, begging him with my eyes to go no further. He shook his head, agreeing that he would stop, but I could tell he knew it all, knew the rest. Knew it as though he'd witnessed it, witnessed all of the ugly aftermath.

Because some weeks after the date, I blundered into the bathroom one morning and screamed when I saw myself. Everywhere, my face, my neck, my shoulders, my back, my arms, I had an angry rash. I screamed when I saw myself in the mirror, and my mother came running.

She was shocked when she saw me and insisted on taking me to the emergency room.

After the doctor examined me—and it was a horrible exam, me

naked, the doctor lifting my arms and peering at my armpits, and everywhere, even the soles of my feet—he asked my mother if he could take photographs. "She'll be anonymous. Nothing that could identify her in the pictures."

Then he asked me if that would be okay. I said yes. Neither my mother nor I asked why.

He called in another doctor and they began photographing with a polaroid. One doctor would lift my arm so that my armpit would be visible and the first doctor would take the picture and wait for it to develop. They moved me around as though I was an inanimate object and my mother sat in the corner of the room and watched, possibly more embarrassed than I was. Afterward, the second doctor took my mother outside and the original doctor spoke to me.

"You have syphilis," he said.

The only thing I could think of was my mother. Did she know? Was the other doctor telling her? Were they close by? Could they hear?

The doctor assured me that wasn't the case. "But," he said, "I have to report this to the health department. You will need to reveal the names of your partners."

Names. Partners. Plural.

"One man. A rape. He didn't even...you know. Finish." My face was burning.

"When was that?"

I told him.

"Did you report it to the police?"

"No." I'd been pretending it hadn't happened. And doing a damn good job of it.

"You'll need a course of penicillin. Several shots. There's no way to avoid it. And when I report this, I'll just say you didn't know the name of the man."

That seemed worse. Only a slut would...what? Jump into bed

with a total stranger? There weren't rape counselors in those days. Or at least the doc didn't mention any.

"Since I'm treating you, you can remain anonymous, but if you don't reveal the man's name, this man could infect other women. And, if untreated, he, and perhaps the women, could die a horrible death years and years down the line."

"What about my mother?"

"My colleague, Doctor Benard, is a dermatologist. He is explaining to your mother that the rash is idiopathic, maybe stress-related. But you should know, the rash will disappear, possibly overnight, but even so, it's important that you get all of the injections. That's what's so dangerous about syphilis."

He left the room and came back with a nurse who carried what looked like a bicycle tire pump. "This is going to hurt. Sorry. And you'll need two more. Do not think you're cured with just this shot, understand?"

The shot went into my bottom for what seemed forever. And yes, it hurt the whole, long while.

I could tell when I saw my mother that the dermatologist hadn't told her I had syphilis. And the next day, like magic, the rash was gone. It had been everywhere, but suddenly, not a trace.

I started reading about syphilis and there was no question that I would go back for the remaining shots and the blood test, a serology, that followed. Without the treatment, syphilis could stay dormant in the body and emerge as madness late in life. A very cruel disease.

I sent a postcard—open for anyone to read--to the health department. It said, "Louis Figulski, 285 Stanley Way, has syphilis." I wrote the word 'syphilis' with a red pen, as huge as the card could accommodate, and mailed it in a box far away from my home. I didn't do it for Louis. I did it for the girls he might penetrate. For years I felt a rush of satisfaction when I imagined postal workers reading and sharing that postcard. Reading and sharing and laughing.

Thinking about all of this had made me forget I was there with Farley. He broke into my reverie. "I'm very sorry," he said. "It's very important that you believe me. You have to stop thinking about me as a murderer. What I am is an avenger."

But how do you avenge something that never happened? And besides, there was no way he could excuse the fury of the blows he'd struck!

The ferocity belied his appearance. He was the original 'mild-mannered man,' if you only considered his appearance. Even if he faced a jury, I doubt they would convict. Unless he showed his other face. A face filled with anger and menace.

Now, he seemed bent on telling me about his own type of clairvoyance. He spoke quickly, as though, at long last, he was sharing his secret with someone other than his wife. "Mostly I experience what is called 'pre-cognition.' I can see into the future most of the time, but occasionally, as with you, I can force myself to see into the past. That is called 'retro-cognition.' That is hard for me. Taxing. Mentally taxing."

Under any other circumstances, I would be thinking he was a screwball, but because of what he knew about me, I knew he had to be the real deal.

"That morning," Farley said, referring to the day of the murder, "I knew the minute I stood on the first step of that staircase out there that my extra-sensory faculties were being engaged. I can't tell you what the feeling is like because it isn't physical. It's like entering a space that is larger than any you can imagine. A kind of hollowness that begins to surround you. And there is a far-off quality to it, as though the space around you goes on forever.

"And sure enough, as I descended the stairs and saw him, I

knew he would harm Leona. I knew it." He closed his eyes and shook his head before looking at me again. "It was unlike what I'd seen before. I saw him from behind! That was a new experience for me. From behind! It was new, but it was absolute."

"But why would he have picked Leona? Did you know the answer to that?"

"Yes, I know it seems inexplicable. But I had a vision, clear as could be, of that boy terrorizing my wife. I couldn't let it happen. Think about it. He was here, at my back stairs, and someday, I knew, he would come here, find Leona and..."

He stopped talking and looked at me. He could see the pity in my eyes, I think, a sign that I was being swayed.

"I decided it was worth the sacrifice," he continued, "and I was willing to pay for the crime without ever saying why I'd done it. But when I found that people assumed I'd acted in self-defense, I was much relieved.

"But also, I knew that evidence to the contrary existed on that phone. The boy's phone. I had seen him with it and at one point he had turned it towards me. You do see that the phone has to be destroyed. Please," he said, "Please will you give the phone to me?" He cocked his head to the side, but despite the innocence of that gesture, his eyes bored into mine. I felt dizzy. Was I being hypnotized?

I was going to say yes.

But the sound of the front door opening and the storm door slamming startled both us. "Yoohoo," Leona called. "Your girls are home."

Sadie came barreling into the room and leapt on Farley's lap. Farley petted her with his bandaged hands. Then Leona appeared. "Oh," she said, looking at me.

Farley tried to lower a wriggling Sadie to the floor. "Leona, you remember Miss Armitage. She came by to check on me."

"How sweet," Leona beamed. "Did he offer you a cookie?" She grabbed Sadie and put her on the floor.

"I was just leaving. I'd like to take one home if that's okay."

Leona went to a cabinet and pulled out a roll of aluminum foil. While her back was to us, Farley made hand gestures which, I assumed, meant he would contact me. I nodded in assent.

Now, Farley and I were locked together. I was about to commit an illegal act at his behest. And what I felt was relief.

When Leona handed me the foil-wrapped gingerbread man, I thanked her profusely. The one I'd already begun to eat was still on the table, decapitated. "This is mine, too," I said, scooping it up and walking toward the front door. The camera still dangled from the strap around my neck.

Farley stood abruptly and he and Leona followed me to the door for goodbyes that seemed to me to be way more profuse and hearty than they needed to be.

I would have a long walk to my car, since I'd entered Farley's property on the Riverwalk and now had to walk down Main Street and then Wilder to get to the Riverwalk parking lot, but that was alright. I had a lot to ponder. Not just Farley's story, his clairvoyance, his access to my own past and what he'd known when he saw Brandon, but my own major omission: I had not told Farley that Brandon was a twin, and I had a powerful feeling that this information was critical.

But if Farley were truly clairvoyant, wouldn't he have known? From what he'd told me, from what I'd seen, he did have some control over his gift. Not all of it, evidently.

CHAPTER TEN

The minute I got back to my home, I began researching twins online. Most of the things I Googled were meaningless. Why would I care that Massachusetts has the most twin births or that the mother of twins is likely to live longer than the mother of a single baby? And why is anyone surprised that twins interact in the womb? The womb is not that big and they're both crammed in there.

On the other hand, I did like knowing that twins are known to invent their own language, a trait that is called *cryptophasia*.

The only serious piece I could find that was close to what I was looking for was a study of conjoined twins who not only read each other's minds but felt sensations of things the other twin was experiencing. One twin would drink and the other could taste it. Or if you tickled one twin then the other would laugh. In that case, the twins had what was called a "thalamic bridge" that linked the thalamus of one girl's brain to the thalamus of the other. When I looked up what the thalamus inside the brain did, I felt a chill. One neuroscientist associated it with feelings of hunger, thirst, rage and aggression.

Rage and aggression.

But Alex and Brandon Sterling hadn't been conjoined.

There was a knock on my door. I knew it was Farley. I picked up Brandon Sterling's phone, now ensconced again in its case, closed my computer and opened the door. I had planned to just hand the phone to Farley, but my ingrained good manners prevailed.

I stepped aside and let him come in. He held a battered leather briefcase. "I want to leave this with you. As a loan. It contains additional proof."

As if I needed it. Nonetheless, I took the briefcase from him and placed it on the floor beside my sofa. My computer was on the coffee table.

He gazed around the room. "Wonderful," he said. "Just wonderful."

You either loved or hated my décor. I didn't even have a name for it. Perhaps eclectic. Perhaps bohemian or 'boho' as it's come to be called. Or *wunderkammer*, house of wonders. I warmed to anyone who approved of it.

"You have architectural pieces," he said, admiring a weathered lion's head that had come off an antique fountain. I showed him what I considered my treasure: a carved wooden horse. "Oh," he said, looking at the wooden piece attached to the rear of it. "It's from a temple, isn't it?"

"Yes. A temple in India." I smiled at Farley. "Do you want a lemonade or tea?" I asked.

"I can't stay. I was just hoping..."

"Oh, yes," I said, handing the phone, in its leather case, to him. Farley looked at the skull imprinted white on the black leather case and made a face. Then he tucked the phone into his trouser pocket.

"The ridiculous password is printed inside," I told him.

"Thank you," he said, and moved toward the door. I stepped

ahead of him and opened the door, watching as he crossed the patio and ascended my front steps. I had pretty much held my breath through the entire exchange. I was relieved now that he and the phone were gone.

Unlike the other homes on my road, my house is sunken to take advantage of its riverfront location. While the others near me had to look down at the river from a cliff, my property sloped politely towards the water, though there was no walkway at the shore. Still, I was positioned high enough so I didn't have to fear a flood, since the property across from me, a dedicated park, was even lower. When the river rose, that was where the water went.

While most of the foliage on my property grew unattended, I'd actually planted the landscaping that surrounded my lap pool, something I'd installed early on. In summer, I swam daily, sometimes just floating on my back admiring the mix of trumpet vine, four o'clocks, plumbago and coral vine. Yes, all my life, I'd craved beauty, however esoteric my definition of it might be. Now, in winter, the rich mix of color was gone.

But still, there was the house itself. The room that Farley had entered, for example. It was wild with bold African fabrics, suede hides, silk, velvets and satins.

I probably learned what I do from watching my mother put clothes and accessories together, through a kind of osmosis. Anyway, it had served me well. And it turned out Miriam, my employer, had been mentored by a designer whose clothes my mother favored.

I have only once met Miriam, the designer who hired me. In person, I mean. She admired what I was wearing and she asked about my background. I laughed and told her I had started choosing fabrics quite early, at the age of three or four.

She was amused and intrigued. She pried the story out of me

and I told it with zeal. It was a funny story my parents liked to tell. My mother was having a sofa reupholstered and had taken me with her to the upholsterer's shop. She sat at a desk sorting through swatches of fabric while I settled down with yet another batch of samples.

My mom says she and the shop owner nearly fell on the floor laughing when they saw me, a toddler, lugging a heavy book of fabric samples to the desk. The book fell, and I sat down beside it flipping from swatch to swatch to find the one I'd seen.

"This one! This one!" I had shouted.

My mom and the upholsterer looked at the swatch I'd chosen and my mother admitted that she liked it. But then I started yelling, "No! No! No!"

"What's wrong?" my mother asked. "Isn't that the one you picked?" I turned the fabric over to display its nubby underside. "This," I insisted.

My mother considered it seriously. "That just might work," she said. "In fact, I like it." It had an earthy appeal. In fact, it looked almost ragged, as though it had been woven in some native hut somewhere.

"I absolutely will not do that," the upholsterer said, all huffy.

My mother straightened. "You will if you want the job." Thus I'd selected my first fabric and my family ended up with a uniquely covered piece of furniture. I should add that everyone who saw our sofa praised it.

The funny thing is, I think this story had a lot to do with the designer hiring me.

And what luck it was! She provided me with enough to live on and more. She calls me her "juxtaposition specialist," and she and I giggled about the ambiguous title when she gave it to me. Still, it is what I use as 'occupation' on my federal income tax forms and thus far--seven years now—the IRS seemed to be okay with it.

She valued what I called my "pairings" and she introduced me to a series of fabric brands who offered their products "to the trade," as they called it. I was suddenly an insider, shown the embroidery of Savoia, for instance. I was admitted into the private world where the finest textiles were envisioned: Peacock Alley, Kerry Joyce, Bailey & Griffin, Stark.

The holidays are my slowest season. There was no better time for all of this recent drama to have happened. including my research into the subject of twins.

But before I sat down at my computer to continue my twin research, I wanted to make a run to the local supermarket. I wanted to clear the deck, so to speak, before I started digging again.

I came out of the supermarket pushing a cart full of food when he called my name. "Eleanor," he said. Then, "Ma'am? Miss Armitage?"

I turned around to find Carl hulking behind me. He got right to the point. "Remember you said you'd go to the police station with me and make them give me my phone back?"

He had me there. "Yes."

"Could you go with me now?"

I thought about my selection of groceries. Did I have anything frozen or that needed to be refrigerated? I didn't. I had paper towels, toilet paper, Febreze, nothing that I couldn't leave in the trunk of my car.

He repeated, "could you?"

I heard myself saying, "sure."

The police station was more or less behind the supermarket. I asked Carl, "Do you want to walk?"

"I got my truck," he said. "You can ride with me." With that, he escorted me to one of those larger-than-life pickup trucks. Fortunately there was a drop down step by the door. I would never have been able to climb in otherwise. I also needed the grab bar by the door. I felt like a monkey.

He smiled at my effort but didn't say anything about how

ridiculous I might have looked. Instead, he asked, "What have you been up to?"

"Oh, some reading, some internet research. How about you?"

He looked over at me, puzzled. "I been at the shop. What else would I be doing?"

"What shop?"

"You didn't see the side of the truck?"

"I guess not."

"When you get out, take a look." He pulled into the visitor space at the station. "You should probably come out of the truck backwards," he advised.

I don't know how far off the ground that truck was, but I felt that I was exiting a two-story building on a ladder. I was laughing at my own lack of physical prowess. Carl came behind me and slammed the truck door when I finally got my feet on the ground.

"See?" he said, pointing at the type stenciled on the door. "Carl's Auto Body. That's me."

I had driven past the place for years. It was a big warehouse and its parking lot was always thronged with vehicles. "Oh!" I said, impressed.

"If you mess up that little car of yours, you know where to bring it," he said proudly.

This time someone was at the front desk, a freckled redheaded young woman in a dark blue uniform. "We're here to retrieve some property," I said. I made my voice as sweet as I could, but I wondered why Carl hadn't spoken. It was his phone. But no, Carl stood there like a statue. "This is Carl Sewicki," I said, indicating him. "The police have his cell phone. I was there when he gave it to one of the officers. This happened on December 21."

The girl's name tag said *Cynthia Oates*. She took notes while I spoke.

"It has a camo cover on it," Carl finally said.

"S-E-W-I-C-K-I?" she asked Carl. "Just a minute," she said, taking her notepad and disappearing into a doorway behind her. There was a glass window, and we could see her inside the room itself. She picked up an old-fashioned telephone, punched two buttons, and started talking into it.

Another young woman, this time in civilian clothes, came out. Carl and I could see the camo-covered phone in her hand. She handed the phone to Cynthia and asked for something. Cynthia frowned and hurried back out to where we were waiting.

"Do you have a receipt?" she asked when she came back in.

Uh-oh, I thought. But when Carl said no, she ran back into the other room, still carrying Carl's phone.

When she came out, she handed him the sheets to fill out. There were three sheets in all to sign and Carl had to surrender his driver's license to be photocopied before he was given the phone. But at the end, Officer Oates said. "Thanks very much for letting the department use this. I'm sorry we didn't get it back to you sooner."

"That's okay," Carl told her.

Outside, Carl thanked me as if I'd had something to do with the phone's return. Rather than clambering into Carl's giant truck again, I told him I'd walk back to my car. Although I was eager to get back to my research, I didn't want to feel as helpless as I felt getting in and out of that truck the first time.

Back to twins. I didn't even put the bag from the grocery store away before I sat down at my computer.

I found a magazine article online titled, "Can Twins Share a Mind?" and one of the pediatric neurologists interviewed was a woman named Rose Menard. I Googled her and found her listed at a prestigious New York hospital. When I say 'listed,' I mean that the entry gave what seemed to be her email as well as a phone number.

So I called and was surprised when she answered the phone. I told her my name and asked if I could get some information from her about twins.

"Twins are fascinating," she agreed.

I told her I was interested in whether or not twins shared thoughts and was surprised when she said that they do. "There have been tests," she said, "with surprising results. And some share sensory impressions as well."

As if I didn't know what that meant, she explained. "If you prick the finger of Twin A, Twin B, in another room, exhibits pain in that finger too."

"Where can I read about these tests?" I asked.

"Oh, there's nothing published. They're anecdotal. Just tidbits that we who specialize in twins find especially interesting. One of the accounts that especially fascinates me is about a boy in Romania. Do you know about 'vanishing twin syndrome'?"

That was a no.

"That's when one of the twins dies in utero and is absorbed by the twin who is born. There's frequently some indication depending on what trimester the absorption began. Well, this Romanian boy had an absorbed twin that presented as a hairy patch on the boy's abdomen."

Creepy, but?

"The boy was seen by a psychiatrist who diagnosed dissociative personality disorder, but in this case it didn't follow the traditional pattern."

"What is that disorder?" I asked.

"It used to be known as multiple personality. But in the case of this Romanian boy, he said he could enter the consciousness of his dead brother at will. Even though the brother didn't exist but for that patch of hair. Researchers verified that the boy's mother had been pregnant with twins, but in the first trimester, one died and was absorbed. The mother insisted that her son had never been told. Does this answer any of your questions?" she asked.

"Well, how about this: What if you had twins who could access each other's minds? Let's say that's a given. My question is, could a clairvoyant person read the mind of Twin A thinking that he was reading the mind of Twin B?" I was inwardly pleading that Dr. Menard not think of me as a nut case.

She laughed. "Let me guess. You're writing a science fiction novel."

Well, I wasn't, but it occurred to me that it was a good cover story. "Screenplay," I told her.

"Don't list me as a consultant, please," she said. "Because I don't know how to begin to answer your question. If you had asked if one twin could access something in the other twin's mind, I'd have said that it's a possibility. But you've inserted a third person, a person with extra-sensory perception. You're veering into The Twilight Zone. It's beyond science, and I am a scientist."

Farley was a scientist too! All of a sudden I remembered the first time I'd encountered him. When he'd shouted, "Science! Ha!" as I was walking away. Was he suggesting something that would connect him and me?

I'd never know. I tuned back into the telephone conversation and asked, "If you were watching a movie, when that was discovered, would you walk out of the theatre?"

"Hmmm. Probably not. Because, if you convinced me that clairvoyance existed, it would be possible. Particularly with my specialty."

Specialty? "What is your specialty, Doctor?"

"Craniopagus twins. Twins conjoined at the head. Specifically, conjoined vertically. And the test of sensory perception that I mentioned? Twin A's finger is pricked and Twin B's finger hurts in the same spot?"

"Yes?"

"That test was conducted after a craniopagus pair had been successfully separated. I don't know if that helps your theory or hurts it."

I lied. "Everything you've told me has helped, Doctor Menard. Thank you so much."

"Be sure to let me know when the movie comes out," she said, hanging up.

But did it help or hurt? The Sterling twins were plain old garden variety twins. Not craniopagus.

CHAPTER ELEVEN

Later that evening I placed a call to Officer Connor Randall.

"This is a nice surprise," he said.

I didn't let him bask in the moment for very long. "I didn't tell you everything. About the murder. About Farley." I waited, but he didn't say anything, so I went on. "I actually had a video of Farley killing that boy. A video that started before the first blow was struck. It's very different from the one the Lost Pines Police sent out. You have to see it."

"I'd like to," he said, but his voice sounded a bit hesitant.

"Tonight. Can you?"

"Did something happen? Are you all right?"

"What happened is that I'm feeling overwhelmed by all of this. Overwhelmed and sorry I didn't tell you about the video last time. I was going to give it to the Sterlings, thinking they'd want to know what really happened, but then, you know, I thought I saw the dead boy and got all freaked out. So can you come? I mean here, to my home?"

"Okay, hang tight. I'll be right there."

"Do you have a pen? I'll give you directions."

"I don't need directions. I'll be right there," he said. "Give me an hour." And hung up.

I hadn't expected it to be over that easily. I was glad that Connor was coming, but not with a romantic sort of feeling. That sort of thing was definitely over for me. But there was something, a sense of safety that I felt. And oddly, a newfound need to share.

I sat on the floor by my front door as the darkness gathered, not turning on any lights. When he knocked, I remained on the floor, but reached up to turn the knob and yank the door open.

"Hey," he said, squatting beside me. "You all right?" He stood and extended his hand. I grabbed it and stood too.

"Don't you have electricity?" he asked, shining a flashlight around the room, then he proceeded to a switch that turned on all the lamps around the room. I watched him as he took it in. "Nice," he said.

He walked over to my favorite thing: the carved wooden horse head that had come from a temple in India. "Very nice," he said.

"You have to suspend your disbelief," I told him, when he asked about the video. "Because this whole thing is as weird as it gets."

"I'm sure it is." He had a smile on his face. A teasing smile. I knew that as I told him the story, that smile would disappear.

I started with my coming on the murder scene, with Carl filming, then the police. I told him about Sadie and how, because of her rooting around, I'd found the boy's phone.

"Did you know for sure it was the boy's?" His voice had hardened. He wasn't teasing any longer. He had switched to cop mode or something close to it. Devil's advocate, perhaps.

"The case had a skull stenciled on it. And his password, written inside the case, was obscene."

"Figures. I don't suppose you'd tell me what it was."

"Not a chance."

"I could arrest you if you don't tell me," he said.

"This is strictly need to know," I said. "But anyway, with that password," at this I blushed a bit, even though I hadn't said the words, 'Nopussy4U,' out loud, "I was able to watch what was on that phone. A video. A video where Brandon is taking a selfie and complaining that his parents were planning to move here and all the while he's talking, Farley is sneaking up on him. Farley attacks him from behind and then kills him."

"That's on the phone?"

"The first blow. The look on Farley's face. Oh, God..." I felt a piercing pain on the bridge of my nose—a sign of impending tears. I tried to hold back, but they broke through nonetheless.

He got up and crossed the room and bent down to me in my chair. Said exactly the right thing. "Shhh. Shhh. You'll get through this. Come on."

"I'm sorry," I said.

"This is heavy duty stuff," he said. "I get it."

He waited until I'd got hold of myself and then stood up. "Can you show me the phone?" he asked.

"I gave it to Farley," I said.

His brow furrowed. "What? Did he threaten you or rough you up or—"

"No. He explained why he killed the boy and asked me to give the phone back to him, and I did. This is where it gets weird."

"O-kay," he broke the word up in the way you say 'okay' when someone has said something you find unbelievable.

"I'm going to tell you what he said to convince me." You're going to think I'm crazy, but I believe him. But first I think we should look at the video."

"You just said..." Connor had a questioning look on his face and it made me laugh.

"I have the video on my computer. I transferred it from the phone." Nora Armitage, computer guru. But I'd learned much from my Electrix expedition and good old Google.

We went into the dining room and pulled two chairs together. Side by side, we watched the video on the computer screen. Connor's only comment was, "Holy shit."

"Again?" I asked? And went back to the beginning.

"Can you make it do slow motion?" he asked.

"Yup."

The third time, I said, "I'm going to mute it when the phone flies out of his hand. "I can't stand that sound." I told him. It was true. The sound of the murder was far more revolting than the sight. I think we get used to seeing pretty realistic murders on television and in the movies, but I'd never before heard what I heard when Farley was hitting Brandon.

After we'd watched it a few more times, I went for the briefcase Farley had left with me. It was a godsend, since otherwise I'd have to tell him Farley had known secret stuff about me. I knew it would sound farfetched, but as I sorted through the memorabilia Farley had left—pictures of grownup children in exactly the occupations he'd predicted—Connor still seemed unconvinced.

"What we saw was homicide," he said.

"Justifiable homicide," I said. "He was defending his wife. It's difficult and I know you won't believe it at first, but really, all these years, he's had this...gift. I guess it's clairvoyance or something, where he...you know, he was a teacher and he encountered lots and lots of children, and some of them, he could look at and know—know with absolute certainty—what was going to happen to them, what they'd turn out to be when they'd grown up.

"And," I continued, "he knew when he saw Brandon that

Brandon was going to kill his wife, Leona. Not just kill her, but torture her, too."

"Oh, boy," Connor said. Clearly, he didn't believe.

"I know, but I believe him. His wife knows he has the gift, but I don't think he told her about Brandon. Until he read Brandon's future, everything Farley had seen had been benign or at least neutral."

"Yeah, well there's one big hole in Farley's story," Connor said, "and that's *why*. Why would this kid from some other town want to torture some old lady he didn't even know existed? And now what? Is Farley going to go after Alex, too?" Connor asked.

"He doesn't know about Alex. I didn't tell him."

"Yeah, well maybe someone from the Great Beyond will let him know." There was more than a hint of sarcasm in his voice.

"But wait," I said. "I found out a lot of things about twins."

I told him about what I'd read and about talking to Doctor Menard. She hadn't agreed with me, but after talking to her, I was convinced that twins had a mystical connection of some kind. "So, see? Twins are so intertwined with each other that Farley may have been reading Brandon's twin brother Alex."

"But Brandon was the evil twin. Alex is the good one," Connor said. "Why would the good twin be thinking something that the bad twin would be more likely to think."

I looked at him and suddenly I knew what had happened. "Oh, my God," I screamed. "Oh, my God."

"Well let me in on it," Connor said.

Oh, my god! What had dawned on me was this: That Farley had caused the whole thing. Farley read Alex's mind and killed Brandon and because of that, Alex, planning revenge, would fulfill the future that Farley saw. "Do you see it? Farley read Alex's mind, like *now*. He was looking into a future that was *now*. Farley could see Alex hurting Leona because Alex is thinking about hurting her *now*."

"This is like the Quaker Oats box thing. He's holding the box and on the box he's holding the box."

"Ad infinitum," I laughed. "That used to drive me crazy. And the Great Silkie legend! Do you know that story? But anyway, that would answer the question of why a boy in Potts would want to come and kill an old lady in Lost Pines."

Connor looked troubled. "The thing is, we have to do something about this. But I cannot for the life of me imagine explaining this to anyone. No one would believe it."

"Maybe we have to scope Alex out and see if Alex really is planning some kind of revenge. But wouldn't he want revenge against Farley? Why would it be Leona he'd want to hurt?"

Connor seemed to know. "Farley hurt Alex by taking away someone Alex loved. So Alex is planning to do the same thing." The tone of Connor's voice said he was taking this seriously, which was a huge relief. But then he said, "Look, I'm a sworn police officer, and I can't ignore a homicide that was captured on tape. I just can't..."

"Please," I begged. "Just wait. Just wait until we figure it out."

"I'm not sure it *can* be figured out."

"Connor, Farley knew things about me. He knew that my parents called me 'Button.' Absolutely no one knows that but me. Well, and now you. And he knew lots more, things I'd never have believed if he hadn't said them out loud. Please wait. Please. I'll..."

"Oh, boy! You'll what?" He reached for my hand.

Ordinarily, I'd have recoiled, but I let him keep my hand enclosed in his own. He squeezed it and then let go, smiling broadly.

"Tell you what," he said. "How about letting me call you 'Nora?'"

I was astonished. Somehow, through our interacting, he'd deduced that I was often called 'Nora,' a more intimate version of my given name. I looked at him in that moment with a mixture of warmth and gratitude. He had pierced my carefully constructed armor and there I was: still whole, still alive.

In a movie, we might have kissed, but something in the way I held myself completely wiped the moment out. Perhaps he'd just realized, as I had, that I'd successfully talked a police officer into covering up a murder.

"Before we go any further," Connor said. "I want to know why you think the people of Lost Pines think you are the town crazy. Really, I want to know."

"Oh, look, forget I said anything. It's stupid and it's boring and it's about someone you don't know and it would take forever to explain."

He was grinning. "Try me."

"Right now?"

"Yes."

I took a deep breath. "Well, there's this contractor in town, Ronald Farron, and I knew he had done some really illegal stuff and..."

"Illegal how?" Connor interrupted.

"There was a nonprofit in town that my friend had started and Ronald Farron got on the board and eventually took it over and sold the property the nonprofit had acquired to himself for way under its actual value.

"Farron had drummed my friend off the board and he basically took everything she had built and nobody cared. After that, the nonprofit didn't do anything, so Farron got the property—a whole city block inside the city limits—and after he paid for it, he got to keep the money he had paid for it, too. It sounds extreme, but Megan just went into a depression that didn't end."

"That doesn't explain why you are the town's crazy person," Connor pointed out.

Had I called myself that? 'Town crazy' sounded worse than pest or troublemaker. But, looking back, I might well have crossed the line. "Megan was my only friend. She was in her 70s when I met her and she was funny and stylish and I loved going over to her house where she had lots of plants and animals, even goldfish. She called it 'life-affirming,' and it was, even though I thought the term was way too trendy.

"But after the Farron thing, she let everything go. It was horrible. The fish died and the plants died and there was dog poop all over the place. I had to call her daughter to help. Even after her daughter kind of got her back together again, she was still obsessed. She talked about the Farron thing all the time to anyone who would listen.

"Ronald Farron had swindled this organization out of maybe two hundred thousand dollars or more and nobody cared. Except Megan and, eventually, me.

"I tried to get the city council to step in, and I spoke up and maybe got kind of shrill at meetings and stuff. I sent Letters to the Editor of our newspaper. I went to the Lost Pines police and tried to get them to do something. I got the way Megan got, unable to talk about anything else. And eventually people would see me and say, 'Oh, no, there's that Armitage woman!' This is a small town, so that's the reputation I got. Pushy, and yes, maybe even crazy, I don't know. It was a couple of years ago, and that's what stuck.

"What about your friend?"

"When Ronald Farron was elected to the city council, she just stopped being Megan. And now she's dead. Sometimes I wonder if she ran out in front of the car that hit her, but that's what happened. She died right there on the street. They didn't even take her to a hospital, just right to the funeral home.

"Who was the driver?"

"Hit and run. Before that, she and I used to go out to lunch and we used to see shows in Austin. After her funeral—which very few people even came to—I just pulled back completely. I love my house and my property, so I didn't want to sell and go somewhere else, but I just withdrew. I go out when I have to, but I keep to myself as much as I can."

"That's pretty bad," Connor admitted. "But I'm glad you told me. I'm glad that now I know."

Once I had started talking about it, I couldn't stop. I added, "And Ronald Farron is ugly, too," I said. "He has this puffy red face and he's fat and he looks kind of like a cherub. But a cherub who sold his soul to the devil. An evil cherub."

I could see the smile on Connor's face—indulgent, maybe tickled by my description.

I went on, "They never found the person who was driving the car, and I don't even think they tried." I was bitter about that, too. "In the movies, they look for pieces of glass and paint scrapings and tire tracks, but not here in Lost Pines."

"When was this?"

"When she was killed? It was fourth of July. Independence Day. Next fourth of July it will be two years."

I felt lighter after telling him. Lighter for having unburdened myself. And Connor didn't seem to think less of me. He seemed, in fact, to understand.

"How's this for a plan?" he asked now. "Tomorrow, we could stop by the Sterling house, check Alex out. Maybe tell the Sterlings we were making a condolence call."

I brightened. "You could say you lost your own brother when you were young."

He looked at me for a long time, then grabbed my shoulders and pulled me toward him. He kissed my forehead and then let me go before I could even object.

"Look. It's complicated enough as it is without me inventing brothers I don't have. Let's think for a bit, okay? Let's get something to eat. What's open this late in Lost Pines?"

CHAPTER TWELVE

We were scarfing down a pepperoni pizza. I was a healthier eater than Connor, but thought I'd let it go.

"If we do go to the police, it should probably be the Texas Rangers," Connor started, but I interrupted.

"You said we wouldn't. Not right now." I snagged a piece of pepperoni with my fingers.

"I didn't mean right now," he said, chewing and talking at the same time. Ordinarily that would have been a major turnoff.

"Anyway," I advised, "not the Lost Pines Police. I tried to give them the phone and they didn't want it."

He cocked his head. "Seriously?"

"Remember? Me? Town crazy?" I admitted.

"I almost forgot," he laughed.

"Seriously. You saw what the newspaper article is going to say about this boy and his murder. Nobody cares, Connor."

He gestured at the last piece of pizza on the plate. "You gonna eat that?" he asked.

"Take it." I felt so comfortable with him. I'd been guarding myself for far too long.

"Do you think this Farley character has some kind of pull with the local police?" he asked me.

"No, it's not that."

"How much do you know about him?"

"Well, I guess nothing."

Connor wiped his face and hands and took out his phone. He poked around on it.

"What are you doing?" I asked.

"You don't want to know."

I reached for his phone and he pulled it out of my reach. "I'm looking up the Great Silkie thing you were talking about. Are you satisfied?"

I was.

It was awkward when we got back to my place. I certainly didn't want Connor to have to drive the forty miles back to Potts. On the other hand, I didn't want him to think that he would be sharing my bed.

He solved the problem nicely, testing my sofa for comfort. "Okay?" he asked.

"Okay."

I spread a lavender flat sheet over the sofa cushions and brought a light green pillow from my own bed. Then I brought in two top sheets and weighed the color choices. I decided on one that was rust. "You'll need a blanket," I said, carrying in a rust and brown Pendleton camp blanket.

"Wow," he said. "Do I get a flower arrangement too?" His tone said he admired what I'd done.

"If you want one," I said. "On the other hand, perhaps you'd settle for a cup of cocoa."

"Seriously?"

"No." My god, I was joking! Teasing! Acting like a woman who has met a man! Not just a man, but what Megan would have described as 'a possible someone.'

"I assume the bathroom is back that-away," he pointed to a hallway.

"Your towels and a washcloth are in there on the vanity. And you don't have to worry about bumping into me. I have my own bath."

"Thanks."

"You're welcome. Goodnight."

CHAPTER THIRTEEN

DECEMBER 29, 2019

In the morning, when I walked into the kitchen, Connor was wearing the same jeans and shirt he'd had on the day before. He was sitting on a stool drinking a Boost. "Ah!" he said. "The princess awakens."

"I know, I know, it's really late." I opened the fridge and grabbed a Boost for myself.

"Is this all you have for breakfast?"

"Usually."

"Well, I think I'd need maybe four of these to get going. But I don't want to deplete your supply."

"How about waffles?" I asked him.

"Too much trouble," he said.

"Not at all." I reached into the freezer and popped two frozen multigrain waffles into the toaster. Then I set a place for him on the counter. I heated the pure maple syrup in the microwave for a moment, then transferred it to a little ceramic pitcher. I unwrapped Irish butter and put it on a plate with a butter knife.

"Thank you. You ought to run a bed and breakfast," he said. "But maybe you do."

"Far from it," I said.

All of a sudden I was much chattier than usual. I elaborated on the work I did for Miriam in New York. "I select fabrics for her clothing collections. She emails drawings to me and I FedEx fabric samples to her. She likes what I pick, usually. Occasionally I have to travel, but not that often."

"Travel to New York?"

"No. Paris, Milan, Stockholm, places like that. Not that often, but whenever she or I hear about something special I might want to see."

He whistled. A sign of appreciation. "Wow. Some job!"

"I know. It sounds exotic but really, except for the two or so months after her drawings arrive, there's not that much to do. But she pays me all year round."

"How did you get a job like this?"

"It's odd. I was in New York, and you know the sort of raggedy things I like to wear, and," I stopped, realizing he had no idea what kind of clothes I was talking about. "Wait!" I dashed into my bedroom and came out with a typical Nora Armitage outfit: a sheer maroon and gunmetal beige plaid jacket bordered with nubby grey. A grey paisley long sleeved top deliberately cut to peek out beneath it. I held up the hanger. "Things like this, not matchy-matchy. Anyway, she—her name is Miriam—came up to me and said she admired the choices I'd made and we just started talking and we went for coffee and then went back to her studio and she had bolts of fabric and I went around combining this and that and the next thing I knew, I was employed. She's a big deal designer, too. I can open just about any fashion magazine and see the wardrobe she designed with fabric choices that I put together right here."

"Are you a designer too?"

I laughed. "She calls me her 'juxtaposition specialist' and that's what I write on my income tax. It sounds fancier that 'fabric put-togetherer.'"

We decided to take his car as well as mine. That made sense. He wrote his address, zip code and all, on a post-it note and gave it to me. "I thought I was following you," I said.

"You can put this in your GPS," he said, "in case we get separated at a light or something."

"I don't have a GPS," I told him. "My car is a 2001."

"Use the map thing on your cell phone," he advised.

"I don't have a cell phone," I admitted.

"You are an intriguing woman," he said, opening the front door. That was when I saw the pickup he had come in. "It's a 1991 GMC Syclone," he explained. "A real prize."

I walked around it. It was horrible. It looked as though someone had painted it green with a brush. There was no tailgate. There was a camper top, but part of one side of it had been broken off. I opened the driver side door and when I did, the inside handle that rolled the window up and down fell off.

"That's the first thing I'm gonna fix," he said.

"Okay," I said, handing the handle to him, "I don't think I'll have any trouble keeping up with you."

Ugly as it was, the little green truck could really move. At times Connor even drove a bit above the speed limit. I imagined him being pulled over. "I'm on the job," he would say, just like on TV. I tried to invent names for his truck: Green Bean, Green Hornet, and so on. I settled on Irish, which the name Connor Randall probably was.

. . .

Off the main highway, we zigged and zagged until I pulled in beside him at a flat-roofed, concrete rectangle painted white. It did not seem to have windows. Could this be where he lived?

"Remember," Connor said, opening the door of my Mercedes, "no judgment."

There was a steel door, and Connor opened it for me. I stepped into a vestibule, and then turned left into his living room. "Oh my God," I said.

Indeed. It was stunning.

The interior was flooded with pot lights. The walls were white and the concrete floor had been stenciled in a black and white pattern reminiscent of Ellsworth Kelly. The furniture was a combination of chrome and tan leather. This was not the plumped up leather you see in cheesy furniture stores; this was really elegant design. The chairs, for instance, had sling seats that were made of a solid piece of thick hide.

I'd have to say the space had an industrial look because of the huge, riveted steel beams, but the effect was softened by accents of thick cut cedar, a wall of open bookshelves and another wall with a huge Texaco sign, edged in rust, probably five feet in diameter.

Connor had gone into the back, I presumed to change, so I shouted. "I'm jealous." While my own home was rife with curated clutter, I did sort of envy the sense of serenity that open space provided. His home was also quite manly.

He came out adjusting the black tie that was part of his gray uniform. "Glad you approve," he laughed.

"I don't just approve, I...I really want to see the rest."

"Now, now," he said. "The rest really is a mess."

"I don't care," I told him, and it was true.

The bedroom was stark, perhaps monastic. The room had no skylight, but Connor flicked a switch and three columns of pot lights went on to illuminate the room. A platform bed with grey linen sheets and a folded khaki-colored blanket at the foot. Beside the bed, two cedar shelves anchored to the wall to serve as bedside tables, and beside them, metal pulley lamps for reading.

Instead of a typical headboard, behind the bed was a free-standing wall. Opposite the bed was a long cedar counter bearing a computer and other office-like things. A large, flat-screen television floated above the desk.

Connor led me behind the headboard wall, where a massive cedar built-in adhered to the other side. It served as a closet and chest of drawers.

Then there was the bathroom, with an antique tin slipper tub and a ringed shower apparatus above. The automotive theme picked up with the rusty front of a gas pump on the wall and a curtain made of many different license plates hinged together vertically over the one small window. The rod was long, so that the curtain could be slid off to the side like a barn door if natural light was required.

If someone asked for a one-word description, I'd have said, "Ingenious." With an exclamation point. To him, I said, "This is wonderful, Connor. How long have you been working on this space?"

He shrugged. "I just did a little here, a little there. It kind of depended on what I came across and how much money I had at the time."

No. I could see the place had not been put together so casually. "And the car theme?"

"That you should know, now that you've seen my truck."

We discussed more than décor. We talked about what we would do when we got to the Sterling house. The funeral for Brandon was over, and, Connor said, a condolence call would seem appropriate. It was good that I'd met the Sterlings, he said, because that way my being there wouldn't seem odd.

"But how did we hook up with each other?" I asked.

"You were lost and I stopped your car to ask if you needed help finding something. When I found out you were looking for the Sterlings, I offered to come along."

"So, will I be in a police cruiser?"

"No, smarty pants. You'll be behind the cruiser in a little Mercedes."

I turned to look back at the room I'd first seen. When I looked at him, he seemed so proud. But he said, "We can't dawdle. It gets dark really early this time of year."

He parked the truck behind the station house and walked over to my car. "Do you mind waiting out here?" he asked. "I won't be long."

When he came back out, he said he had some news. "Word is that the Sterlings are all but celebrating the demise of their troublesome son."

"Oh, you're kidding."

"No. Like I told you, he was a handful. He was well known to all of us here and even the Hemings County sheriff. Not just a troublemaker. A cruel kid."

I thought of the still pictures on Brandon's phone. I hadn't copied any of them. I didn't think I'd want to tell Connor about them either.

All the way to Grimes Road and the Sterling home, my fear grew. I was sorry that Connor and I had taken separate vehicles. It would have helped a lot to have been able to talk to him along the way.

He pulled the cruiser all the way up the driveway and I pulled up behind him. The Escalade was parked beneath the covered structure. A small red coupe was parked next to it. Connor waited for me and, together, he and I walked up the wide front stairs.

. . .

Janice Sterling opened the door before Connor could even knock. "Officer Randall," she said. "And..." looking at me as though trying to recall why it was that I looked familiar.

"Eleanor Armitage. I was with you at the Lost Pines police station."

"Oh, yes. Come on in."

Their living room was beautiful, with Mission furniture complimenting the Craftsman style of the home. Their fireplace was flanked with solid oak built-ins with glass doors, and the fireplace itself had those old carved earthen-colored tiles. Somehow, although the home looked right for Janice, it didn't seem right for Ray.

All of the Christmas presents and the tree that I'd noted when I'd peered through the windows were gone, though I detected a faint whiff of pine.

Ray Sterling walked into the room. Janice intercepted him, reminding him of who I was. He didn't offer to shake my hand but shook Connor's. "Get you a beer?" he asked.

Although I felt I hadn't been included in the offer, we both demurred.

"I ran into Miss Armitage here downtown just a while ago," Connor said. "She seemed lost. But when I found out she was looking for y'all, I thought I'd show her the way and come with her to offer my condolences, too."

"That's a lie!" A voice from a stairwell leading to the basement. Alex emerged. "Mom, that's the lady I saw. She was looking in the windows. That's the same car outside. So, there's no way she was lost," he aimed that last bit at Connor.

"Well, son," Connor said, "maybe she didn't remember the way. She doesn't live in Potts, you know." He pointed at the stairwell. "Is your room down there?" he asked. "Maybe you and me could talk a bit in private."

Oh, no! He was leaving me alone with Ray and Janice! Oh, no! But strange to say, nothing in my voice indicated the panic I was feeling. "As Officer Randall told you, I wanted to extend my sympathy. You weren't here when I first came, and..."

"Thank you," Janice said. "Let's sit down."

"I didn't realize Brandon had a brother," I lied.

"He's a twin, actually," Janice said. She looked around for Ray, but he had already left the room. Janice's husband, in every situation I'd observed, was a pig.

Something in my facial expression must have conveyed that, because Janice said, "You'll have to forgive Ray. All of this has been too much for him." Tears filled her eyes.

"I'm sorry," I said, meaning it.

Janice was crying now. "When he married me, they were such cute kids. He didn't know all this would happen. I can't blame him for being furious."

"But he should help you. Comfort you. He shouldn't be mean to you," I said.

"He has his reasons," she said.

I couldn't think of anything to say, so I just sat there, dumb.

She kept fidgeting in the silence, but I didn't know how to break it. Finally, she did. "Before we ever met, Alex and Brandon were attached to each other, head to head. I didn't tell Ray, because the surgery had been years before and you couldn't tell and none of the articles about the operation said that it was us. But when Ray found out, he said he'd married into a family of freaks."

So they had been conjoined! Conjoined at the head, too! "How did Ray find out?"

"I kept all the newspaper articles. He found them and he figured it out, I guess from the dates or just because I kept the papers. He went ballistic." She got up, went to one of the built-ins and pulled a brown paper envelope out. "Here. Take them," she said. "I don't know why I kept them. Maybe I was hoping I could tell him one day."

She gave me a baleful look. "I just couldn't find the right time. And I didn't want the boys to find out."

"They didn't know?"

"No. We were living in Cincinnati when they had the operation. But I cut out everything I could find about it. I don't know why I did. You can't imagine what it was like to decide. All I kept hearing was how risky it was. But the way they were attached had a very high success rate. Still, signing the permission form..."

She looked as though she was reliving the moment of decision. "The operation took 20 hours. There were smaller surgeries to prepare for the big operation. It was something I thought of with pride. But when most people hear about it, they think it's an unbearable horror."

"Their father left me after they were born. They were in the hospital for two weeks and he never went to see them. He moved out the day they were coming home. He said he couldn't stand being in the same house with them. And he treated me as though he couldn't stand me, either. I was a freak and his kids were freaks. Just the way Ray felt when he found out."

"But Ray stayed," I said, thinking that would indicate that Ray loved her.

Her voice went flat. "I'm the one with the money," she said.

I fell silent again. She looked as though she felt sorry for me. "Let's just drop it," she said, wiping her eyes, sniffing slightly, and mustering a weak smile.

"How's Alex holding up?" I asked. In part I was hating myself for not pursuing the conjoined twin topic the way a seasoned investigator might have done. But it had wreaked so much havoc and who was I to be digging around? It wasn't as though I was Leslie Stahl or some other reporter. Besides, I now had the envelope full of the articles about Alex and Brandon and, if I had any further questions, I could always call Dr. Rose Menard.

I found myself wondering if Alex and Brandon had been the separated twins who had felt the pin pricks that Dr. Menard had mentioned. That would be something.

Janice shook her head. "I don't know. Alex seems angry, too."

I was initially baffled by what she said. I had all but forgotten that I'd asked about Alex a moment before.

"But that's one of the stages of grief, anger, so it's understandable," she said in defense of her son.

I knew of the Elizabeth Kubler-Ross book, of course. I think anger is the first stage. I wondered if she was in the final stage: acceptance.

As if to answer that, Janice said. "It's easier knowing that Brandon was up to no good when it happened. Do you understand that? It's easier. I only wish he hadn't died. I wish he had just finally learned his lesson."

Her face twisted in anguish. "This sounds terrible," she said, "but I don't know what would have happened—what I would have done—if it had been Alex who was dead."

Fortunately, Connor came bounding up the stairs. He addressed Janice. "I left my card with Alex," he said. "Told him he could call me any time. I know what it's like. My best friend had a brother die and it hit him really hard." He avoided looking at me when he said this. He was using a version of the lie I'd suggested.

"Look," he went on. "We've kept you long enough. Please tell your husband how sorry both of us are."

I stood up and followed him to the front door, as did Janice.

"Thanks, officer," she shook his hand. Then she turned to me and gave me a hug. The envelope was crushed between us. When we pulled apart, I saw that she had closed her hands over the envelope. She stared down at it, her eyes moist.

"Maybe you should keep these?" I ventured.

"Maybe so."

I released my hold on the envelope. I don't know whether I meant it or not, but at that moment I said, "You did something very difficult. You deserve to be proud."

"Thank you," she said, her eyes riveted to mine.

"What was with that envelope?" Connor asked. We were outside now. The sky had turned a dismal shade of grey.

"She was going to give me all the articles about separating Alex and Brandon. Then she changed her mind."

"Separating? What do you mean?"

Oh, that's right. Connor didn't know. "It turns out Brandon and Alex were conjoined twins, Siamese twins, born attached to each other. They were attached at the head. The operation to separate them was a success. And they're a piece of her past. She should keep those things."

"What do you mean, 'they were attached at the head'?"

"They were conjoined twins, Siamese twins. I'm thinking that's why they could share thoughts. You know, the thoughts that Farley could read."

Connor didn't say anything until we got to my car. Then, he didn't bring up any of what I'd just told him. "Okay," he said. "Do you think you know the way back to my place from here?"

"I'll follow you," I told him. It occurred to me that the shortest day of the year, the Winter Solstice, had just passed. That seemed good. I watched as he turned his headlights on. I did the same and drew Slick up behind him. I would let him stay a few lengths in front of me, I thought, so he couldn't accuse me of tailgating him.

CHAPTER FOURTEEN

We were back at Connor's place. I think we both felt we couldn't talk about any of this in public. "I didn't get a good vibe from Alex," Connor began. "He's like a cocked pistol, if you ask me."

"But what could he do? What would he want to do?"

"He might want to do what Farley saw him doing. Get even. Take something away from Farley the way Farley took Brandon away from him."

"Leona."

"I'm afraid so."

"But how would he know where Farley lives? How would he know Leona even exists? And he's here in Potts, forty miles away, and he's too young to drive."

"That stuff is easy enough to find out. I mean, he knows Farley's name. He could check with the county appraisal district and get the address. And maybe Farley and Leona both own the house, so now he would know Leona exists. And as for driving, I could drive when I was twelve. And there's always hitchhiking."

"Let's go back to Lost Pines," I said. "And *you* can tell the Lost Pines police. I won't even go. I'll wait for you at my place and..."

"There isn't anything the police can do. Alex hasn't shown himself to be a threat. And also, we'd have to tell the police the whole story. Think about that for a minute."

"But..."

"And," he went on, "if Farley goes to jail, where would that leave Leona? She'd be alone. More vulnerable than ever."

Was Connor changing sides? Was he thinking Farley had a righteous motive? I couldn't tell by looking at Connor's face. All of a sudden I said, "I hate this. A week ago, my life was great. Now, I'm in the middle of this massive mess."

He laughed. "Cheer up, girl. You did meet me."

I looked at him as seriously as I could. It was time to set him straight. "Connor, I am not a candidate for anything, you know, romantic. I don't go out with men. If you must know, I'm..."

The look in his eyes—affectionate, amused—never changed. But he raised his eyebrows. "Are you telling me you're L-G-T-B-Q?" he asked. I think he expected me to laugh.

"L-G-T-B-Q-A," I said it forcefully, emphasizing the last letter. "I'm asexual. And happily so."

He reddened slightly and narrowed his eyes. Other than that, he didn't look at all flustered, but he did change the subject. "Whatever you say. So let's get back to business. What do we do now? What's our plan? Or is this investigation over?"

I stared at him. I think my mouth was hanging open. Was this investigation over?

Was he just going to dismiss what I'd told him? I had never said anything that personal, that revelatory, to anyone and was he just not going to respond to it? I felt the anger inside me bubble towards the surface. I had to get out of there.

"I know what I'm going to do," I shrieked. "I'm going to think about it at home. That's what I'm going to do."

I stormed outside, got in my car and was surprised that the keys were still in the ignition. I almost hit the back end of Connor's stupid truck as I backed out.

I roared away, and in about five minutes realized I was traveling over 100 miles per hour. I immediately slowed down to 75 and exhaled. Maybe I overreacted. Maybe Connor hadn't fully heard what I said. Or hadn't processed it.

Maybe he was embarrassed and changed the subject because he didn't know how to react.

I remembered a boy in one of my art classes telling me that when he'd told his mother he liked boys, she said, "That's ridiculous" and they never discussed it again. He said it hurt more than if she'd called him names. People's reactions differ, I'd told him.

As I pondered this, I pulled over to the side of the road. Maybe I should go back. Maybe I should apologize. Maybe...maybe... maybe... I saw headlights approaching in the rear-view mirror. As soon as my car could be seen, the car slowed and pulled over, coming up the shoulder toward me.

I gunned the engine and sped away. If it was somebody thinking I was in trouble and trying to help, fine, they could see I didn't need any help. And if it was someone who meant me harm, well, *Catch me if you can.*

I went up over 100 again. It felt good. There was something freeing about it. I was even tempted to engage the cruise control, though I had the good sense not to. But then I saw a convenience store up ahead. It was like a mirage in the gathering dark.

Well, I did have to go to the bathroom.

I pulled into the lot, parking off to the side in the shadow of the building. I didn't want the clerk to see Slick. Sometimes people see it and get the idea that I'm rich. Sometimes I've been panhandled because of the car, one guy even argued, "With a car like that, you can't part with a twenty?"

But I could have parked in the doorway itself and the attendant wouldn't have noticed. He was sitting on a tall stool, engrossed in a magazine. When I came out of the rest room, I wanted a peppermint patty and wondered if I could break his concentration.

The answer was yes, I could. But he didn't make eye contact with me at any time during the transaction. I wondered if he owned the place.

I had locked the car, so I fished through my bag for the familiar feel of the car key. I put the peppermint patty on the roof while I searched. I wasn't finding the key, so I stepped into the light and peered inside the purse.

Success. I was at the driver's side door when a body crashed up against me from behind. He had smashed me hard against the car door and knocked the breath out of me. I screamed. Then I knew I had to spend my energy doing more than screaming.

He grabbed my arms and I tried to shake his hold away, But he didn't let me go. Instead, he placed a hand over my mouth and jammed himself in even closer.

I caught a glimpse inside the lighted store and saw the clerk, absolutely unaware. He never once looked up.

He pulled me away from the car and then shoved me back against it again.

Then, even more upsetting, he pressed the lower part of his body against my buttocks. I couldn't believe it. He had an erection and I could feel it bulging against my back side. I could hear him breathing, too. Although I was a long way from high school, I remembered our gym teacher, Mrs. Barr, telling us what to do if ever we were grabbed from behind.

In quick succession, I slammed the heel of my boot down on his instep. Then I flung my elbow back as hard as I could into his stomach. His grip on me lessened and I immediately spun around to face him, bringing my knee up as hard as I could against his testicles.

He crumbled onto the asphalt surface of the parking lot. But even with his head down, I could see it was Alex Sterling, holding his crotch and hollering in pain.

Before I could think of what to do next, a black and white sheriff's car made a U turn and pulled up beside the fallen boy and me. A deputy got out. He wore a cowboy hat and a khaki-colored shirt and pants.

"What's going on here?" he asked. He looked down at the boy and said, "Brandon Sterling. Sweet Jesus, what now?"

Alex was moaning now, oblivious of the deputy and me.

"No, officer," I said. "Brandon is dead. This is his brother, Alex. It's all right, really. He tried to get my attention and I misunderstood and, sort of kneed him. Down there."

I have no idea why I didn't tell the officer what had really happened. Maybe the boy's youth made me feel sympathetic. Or maybe it was because he had just lost his brother. Or maybe I just didn't want to involve someone from law enforcement and turn his stupidity into something criminal.

"I want to see his ID," the deputy said. It was as though the deputy didn't believe that this wasn't Brandon. But why wouldn't someone in police work already know? "I been up in Oklahoma visiting family," he said. "But that Brandon kid was still alive and kicking when I crossed out of Texas."

Alex sat up.

"Got ID?" the deputy said.

"No," Alex said.

"Did you hear what she just told me?" the deputy asked.

"Yeah."

"Is that your story, too?"

"Yeah. My brother got killed," he said. "You can check your radio."

The deputy mumbled something about being sorry for his loss. But then his voice went back to normal, which I would call a bark. "And you two were here in this little bitty car?" He referred to Slick.

I said 'Yes' as Alex said 'Yeah.' Alex stood up and winced.

"Well, what's your name, ma'am? Can I see your driver's license?"

"Sure thing," That was when I saw that my purse had spilled its contents onto the hood of the car. I fished through the mess on the hood, found my wallet, removed my license and handed it to the deputy.

He examined my credential pretty carefully and handed it back to me, picked up my satchel and started putting the things he found back into it. It seemed ridiculous, all that I had. Receipts. Two change purses. A paperback, a pack of chewing gum, a lip gloss, a hairbrush, a comb. The deputy made a show of holding each item in the air to examine it before dropping it back into the satchel. What is it with men and women's purses? Just because they don't carry anything, they don't have to act as though what we carry makes us crazy or something.

As soon as he'd finished with my purse, he handed it to me and addressed Alex. "Alex, given that this lady kneed you in the balls, do you want to file a complaint?"

Alex looked at me sheepishly.

The deputy went on. "What she did to you is assault. Now you didn't do anything to her first, did you?"

Was he kidding? Did the deputy think I would knee someone in the groin without provocation?

"I was just trying to get her attention," Alex said.

Right. By slamming up against me and then getting a goddam erection.

But Alex and I looked at each other, both of us silently agreeing to the lie.

"I overreacted," I said.

The deputy handed me my purse. "Sorry," he said. Then he spoke to Alex again. "Real sorry about your brother," he said. "I didn't know."

"That's okay," Alex said.

"Now, son, do you feel you want to go to the emergency room in Lost Pines and have them take a look at you?"

"No, I'm fine," Alex said.

"Well, then, you two. We don't have to take this any farther. You two have a good night. And stay out of trouble." He pointed at Slick's roof. "And don't forget your candy."

"Goodnight," Alex and I said in unison. We watched the deputy drive off back toward Potts.

"I just wanted to talk to you," Alex told me. "I wanted to know why you were looking in the windows of our house. I wanted to know whatever you knew, you know, about Brandon."

"But you—when you pressed against me, you..." I couldn't even say it.

"I know. It just happened. I don't know why. It just did."

Was he a rapist in the making? Or just a teenaged kid who had his groin pressed up against a woman's backside and therefore became overwhelmed by his hormones?

"Please don't tell anyone," Alex pleaded.

"Okay. But how did you get here? How did you find me?"

"I followed you. In my mom's car. It's over there." He pointed at a small red coupe. The same coupe I'd seen at the Sterling house.

"I drive it a lot. They just don't know that I do. They think I'm downstairs studying or something."

They. He meant his mom and dad, Janice and Ray Sterling. I wondered how Ray treated him.

"I was the reason they hated Brandon so much. They kept comparing him to me. I could get away with anything, because

Brandon was the one that always got blamed. And Brandon just took it, too. Didn't try to rat me out, ever."

I took a deep breath. I think he was saying that Brandon wasn't the only evil twin. But really, I didn't want to know. "I was there right after Brandon got killed. I don't know how it started or anything. What I've been told is that Brandon tried to rob Farley Clement or something, and Farley fought back."

"Yeah. Like some little old man could take Brandon." He clearly didn't believe it could happen.

"I don't know. Maybe fear took over and he found the strength. People do that."

"I think you're lying," he said.

We both just glared at each other. I was the first one to turn away. I opened the door to my car and got in. "I have to get home," I said. "You probably ought to do the same."

"That's the last place I want to be," he said. There was no belligerence in his voice.

"You have your mom's car. Go home." I closed the driver side door. I turned the key in the ignition and, for the first time ever, Slick wouldn't start. There was nothing. Not an attempt to grind, not a click, nothing.

I just sat in the car, bewildered by its lack of response.

Alex rapped his knuckles on the window. I reached for the switch to open it, but of course it didn't work.

I pushed the car door open and he stepped back to let me out.

"I think you left your lights on. They were on when you went into that cop's place and they were on when you went into the store, I mean. Hey, look, I can take you home, come on. Unless you want to call somebody."

I left my lights on? And I hadn't noticed? And Alex, evidently, was following me? Dear God, what was happening to me? I never had left my lights on before and anyway Slick beeps when things like that happen, keys, lights, brake.

"Did you hear me?" Alex said. "I can take you home."

"Oh, right. I really want you to know where I live."

"It's easy to find that stuff out. I already know Farley and Leona Clement's address."

I tightened when I heard him say that. But then I thought, maybe I should let him drive me home. Maybe I could tell him something that would appease the anger and urge to avenge his brother's death. The problem was what I could say that would accomplish that. "Okay, take me home," I said. "But I want to tell the clerk what I'm doing. I don't want them to tow my car away." I started back toward the store.

It occurred to me I ought to ask the clerk to call the police, but that would probably mean the sheriff's deputy who had recently left would come back. So I just said my car has broken down and I'd be back for it tomorrow.

"You need push?" the clerk asked. He hadn't even put the magazine down but spoke to me over it, slumped on his stool.

"No. My friend out there will take me home. Thanks."

"Okay," he went back to his reading.

CHAPTER FIFTEEN

I was tense, confused and fearful in the passenger seat of Alex's car, but not because I thought the boy would harm me. No. I was afraid of my reaction to the way he attacked me, pressed me up against my car from behind. Yes, it was because of his erection.

Not because he, Alex, had felt desire, but because, although my initial reaction had been violent, now, in the car, pondering it, I felt, well, angry, of course, but something else as well. Not an attraction to Alex, of course, but a little flicker of something softer. I did not wish to think about this. I did not wish to feel anything but dead down there. And then I was embarrassed when I realized the last time I'd felt any pleasure within my body was on the way to Louis Figulski's house, when I knew we'd be making out. A shrink would probably say that this was the reason I focused so much on external things. Clothes. Décor.

Ironically, I'd just told Connor I was asexual. And now I pretty much knew I wasn't.

What if the night with Louis had been different? What if I'd experienced pleasure instead of fear? What would that have changed?

Or what if I'd fought him, punished him for what he'd said. Taken his belt and lashed him across the face with it. Lashed him more than once. Lashed him the same way he'd slapped me, over and over. I almost laughed, thinking about it. A cruel laugh at that.

"You okay?" Alex asked, pulling me out of my little fantasy.

"Why?"

"You're making these little noises. I don't know. And you're kind of jerking around."

I looked over at the boy. For a moment, I understood the satisfaction of envisioning revenge.

"I'm okay," I assured him.

I let my mind drift to Connor and the way I'd left him. When I thought that I might not see Connor Randall again, I was bereft. We'd had an ease between us. And his home! It said so much about him.

Alex interrupted. "Where do I go up here?" The road ended in a tee.

"Right," I said. "Turn right. And stay on the frontage road."

He turned right and then pulled into a parking lot in front of a fast-food restaurant. "Just give me your address and your zip code. I've got GPS and I might as well use it."

Inwardly, I cursed technology, but I gave him what he'd asked for. Every time the smarmy female voice told him what turn to take, I hated the GPS thing more.

When we got to the top of my driveway, the voice said, "You have reached your destination." Although my home was some distance from the road and the driveway was unlit, I told Alex I'd get out where we were and walk the rest of the way.

"No," he said. "I'm coming in. I need to know whatever it is you know about that old man and his wife and about how Brandon, you know, died."

I thought of the video on my computer. Oh, I hoped Alex would never see it. If he did, I was sure he'd murder Farley and Leona as well.

"Okay," I said. "Turn down here."

The headlights of the little red car illuminated the stumps of dead ragweed along the drive. Alex harrumphed as though he disapproved. But when he got in range of my front stairs and the motion-powered lights kicked on, he said, "Wow!"

I had a remote that turned the lights on inside the house, but I'd left it in my car, so I couldn't put on that particular display. Still, I felt proud. I always felt proud when showing someone my home for the first time.

I had a push button doorknob that used a combination so I wouldn't have to bother with a key. As I entered the code, I wondered if Alex would memorize the keys I'd hit.

When I flipped the light switch inside the door, Alex looked at the room and said, "Nice! This is really nice!"

I appreciated that he liked the house, but he seemed so surprised, I couldn't help wondering what he'd expected of me. Did he think I'd live in a pigsty?

He pointed at an enormous painting above the fireplace. "Is that you?" he asked. It was a painting of my mother in a formal dress, ice blue. She'd met my father that night.

"It's my mother," I said, and I felt myself smiling, which of course, I hadn't planned.

"You look like her. Except for what you're wearing."

I almost laughed out loud. He was talking about my Lagenlook layers, some deliberately tattered. Sometimes I took it to extremes, like today, when I carried a huge canvas messenger bag as a purse, even though I had several beautiful leather purses in my closet.

"Sit down, Alex. Do you want a soda or something?"

"I'd like water," he said.

I returned with an uncapped bottle of Topo Chico. "Do you want a glass?" I asked. I knew he'd say no. I sat across from him and watched him take a small sip, followed by a glug. It made me laugh.

"What?" he asked.

"Nothing." He really was just a kid.

"Brandon had a cell phone," he said. "The police told my parents that they never saw it. I thought maybe I'd go down to where it happened and look for it myself."

The place where the murder occurred. It was adjacent to Farley and Leona's gate. And within that gate were the stairs that led to their home. Except that Alex didn't know that. Even if he had their address, it would say that they lived on Main Street. He wouldn't be aware that that end of Main backed up to the Riverwalk.

But strange things had been happening. Maybe Alex would feel a compulsion to walk over to that gate and mount the stairs. A feeling that even he wouldn't understand.

"I'm sure they really swept that area," I said, remembering the hubbub. And Farley had looked for the phone as well.

"I don't care," Alex said. "Could we go there tomorrow?"

"Tomorrow?" I had a hint of hysteria in my voice. Was he planning to spend the night here?

"I can sleep in my car," he said.

I knew that I ought to say no, that that was a ridiculous idea, but the alternative was to put him on my sofa the way I had let Connor stay. I just couldn't imagine doing that. "Okay," I said. "I'll give you some blankets and a pillow."

And once I did, out he went into the night.

. . .

At about three in the morning, I heard banging on my front door. I grabbed a robe and went to answer it. Maybe Alex had to use the bathroom, I thought, opening the door wide.

And there, indeed, was Alex, his arms behind his back, in handcuffs, I presumed. Behind him was Connor, in his uniform. "This kid says you knew he was here." Connor's demeanor was stern, which I'd never seen before.

"I did," I said, and stepped aside so the two of them could come in.

Connor unlocked Alex's cuffs and wagged his finger at him. "I'm taking these off for now," he said, "but you better believe they'll be going back on if you make one bad move." With that, he and Alex sat across from me.

"Here's what happened," Connor told me. "Janice Sterling called me and said this kid here was missing, and he'd taken her car. So I drove around looking and then started up the highway, but when I passed that convenience store, I saw Slick."

"Who's Slick?" Alex asked.

"That's what I call my car," I told him. Alex rolled his eyes and I tried to suppress a smile.

"When I asked the clerk inside the store what he knew about the car, he told me you left it there because the car wouldn't start and that he had seen you getting into a little red car," Connor continued. "I didn't know what to think. Like, did Alex kidnap you or what? So I drove here and, sure enough, when I looked inside the car, there he was."

"The clerk saw me?" He had never looked up from his magazine!

"That's what he said."

"Is Alex under arrest?" I asked.

"Beats me," Connor said. He turned to Alex. "I could arrest you for car theft," he threatened. "Except your mom probably wouldn't press charges." Then he turned to me. "She didn't even want his dad to know. And I assume the kid didn't hurt you, coerce you or anything."

I felt my face redden when I thought of the way Alex had flattened me against my car, but I said, "No, he didn't." I didn't look at Alex when I said it. I wondered if Connor noticed. When I looked back at Connor, he was regarding me with suspicion, but evidently decided not to pursue it.

"So what's going on here?" Connor asked.

"Alex wanted me to take him to the Riverwalk tomorrow morning so that he could look for Brandon's cell phone."

"I see," Connor said, his eyebrows lifted a bit. I knew he was thinking that I'd already given the cell phone to Farley. "Well, let's all three of us get some sleep and go over there in the morning." He looked at me for approval.

"Okay."

"So...." Connor wondered.

I adopted my bossiest voice. "You take the sofa," I said to Connor, and to Alex, "and you sleep on the floor. I'll barricade myself inside the bedroom."

Thank God they both laughed at my little joke. I went to the linen closet and opened the door. "Bedding's back here. Help yourselves. And goodnight."

CHAPTER SIXTEEN

DECEMBER 29, 2019

I was in and out of sleep, but pretty much in when the frantic pounding on my bedroom door sunk in. "Nora, Nora," Connor was shouting. I unlocked it and he all but fell inside.

"The kid is gone," he said.

I was too woozy to fully comprehend what that could mean.

Connor realized that. "Get dressed. But hurry. You have to show me where that Farley character lives."

I waited for him to leave the room and tore my nightgown off and pulled on an old crinkle dress that I used for household chores. I wasn't wearing anything underneath, but at that moment I didn't care. I pulled my boots on and ran out to find Connor coming back inside the front door. "Car's gone," he told me.

I'd never been in a police cruiser before, but it was pretty much like any big American car. Of course there was a massive shotgun on a rack behind our heads and a solid-looking wire partition between the front and rear seats.

I told Connor where to turn and we approached the Clement house. The Christmas tree lights must have been on, because we could see an incongruous rosy glow coming from within. The front door was wide open but the aluminum storm door, mostly glass, revealed the interior of the house.

Sadie, their little Jack Russell, was outside on the front stoop, jumping up and down. She wasn't barking, but she was clearly intent on getting back in.

"Stay in the car and use this," Connor ordered, handing me a cell phone. And just then, we heard Leona scream. Connor got out and moved stealthily up the front walk. Sadie turned toward him and started barking. I called 911, rattled off the address, and opened the door on the passenger side, rushing to Connor's side.

"Let me get the dog," I whispered. It was then I saw that Connor had drawn his gun. It was black and looked menacing. It was pointed down at the ground.

I picked Sadie up and she wriggled in my arms. She was quiet again, however. "Good girl, good girl," I kept whispering, holding her tight against my chest.

Connor opened the storm door and kept it from closing until I could come inside. Sadie was wriggling more furiously and I wasn't sure I could hold onto her, but I did.

We couldn't see Leona, but we could hear her whimpering.

Farley's body was lying in a heap in the hall. I watched Connor step over him, moving toward the sounds that Leona was making.

I bent down to where Farley was and Sadie wiggled away from my grasp. She started to nose around Farley's face, licking him. He groaned softly, so I knew he was alive. I stood and stepped over him the way Connor had.

The boy, his back to us, was jabbing Leona with something. He would poke and then stab and twist, poke, stab and twist. He was shouting whenever he stabbed, but not when he jabbed. I looked back at Sadie and she stayed there with Farley, nuzzling him, licking his face.

The Christmas tree was on its side and in the glow of the lights strung around it, I could see tinsel, ornaments and shiny bits of smashed glass everywhere. Leona was sprawled next to the branches of the tree. She wore a long-sleeved light-colored nightgown, and splotches of bright red blood seemed to be everywhere: her shoulders, her left breast, her stomach, her thighs.

I can only describe Alex as hyped up. He was darting in and out, toward Leona and away, the way a boxer would. He suddenly became aware of Connor's presence and his frantic movement paused.

Alex turned to face Connor, a bloody corkscrew in his hand. His eyes were big and round and dead. As though, if I tried to make contact with him, I couldn't. I wouldn't be able to break through to him in the state he was in.

Connor could have shot him at that moment but did not. Instead, he lunged at Alex and the two fell onto the downed tree and began fighting. I saw Connor's gun fall and land near Leona. *Grab it, grab it,* I tried to instruct her mentally, but she seemed too dazed to notice anything, the gun, me, even the fistfight.

I moved past the fighting and picked up the gun but doing that was useless. Connor and Alex were moving too fast for me to have safely taken a shot. I examined the gun and pictured myself bludgeoning Alex with it, saving Connor. At that moment, I knew I would have been able to do that.

Behind the two combatants, I saw Farley stir and begin crawling towards the fray. But with those bandaged hands, what could he do? Sadie, oddly, was sitting and observing, as if she knew that this was a time to be quiet.

Farley thrusted his arms out and, sure enough, began beating on the legs of the boy with his bandaged hands. The boy kicked back at Farley, and when he did, Connor grabbed him, jerked him off balance, and tossed him on the floor.

Connor dropped to one knee, flipped Alex over so that he was face down and in one sweeping move, locked handcuffs on Alex's wrists.

Farley got close to the boy again and tried to pummel him, but again, Connor pulled him away. "We've got him," Connor told Farley. "Ease up."

I stooped next to Farley and laid a hand on his shoulder. He shook me off, stood, and backed away. Connor had moved to Leona. He began examining Leona, gingerly holding his hand over the spots of blood to get some idea of the wounds beneath the flannel. The cloth was sticking to the blood, so he looked at me as if to say that he didn't dare try to pull the fabric away.

We heard sirens. *It's about time,* I thought. Farley had moved behind me and I thought everything would now be okay.

It wasn't.

I didn't see Farley pulling the bandages off his hands. I'm not even sure how he did it. But immediately, there he was, bare-handed, clutching the menacing black gun. His hands looked small and white, almost undeveloped and weak, but they were steady.

He didn't hold the gun with both hands, the way cops do on television. No. He held the gun sideways and close against his body nearly at his waist. His face had that same fierce look I'd witnessed on the Riverwalk when he had murdered Brandon Sterling.

Now, right in front of Connor and me, Farley aimed at Brandon's twin, Alex, lying helpless on the floor. Surely, he wouldn't shoot.

Alex, on the floor, lifted his head and shoulders and faced Farley. He stayed that way, though it must have taken enormous strength to do that with his body flat on the floor. I couldn't help but think of a serpent.

I glanced at Connor, and he looked hard at Farley, but he was poised, I think, to move forward and knock the old man over. We all froze in our positions for what seemed a long, long time. The tableau was broken by a loud explosion. Alex's head and shoulders immediately dropped to the floor and a small concentric red circle appeared in Alex's temple. Blood began to pool beneath the boy. Alex's body moved, jerking. And then the boy made a gargling sound and was still.

Connor walked over to Farley, who still had the gun in his hand. My heart stood still. Connor wrapped his fingers around the muzzle of the gun and Farley, who looked normal again, surrendered it.

Leona was limp, but breathing and moaning. The blood spots on her nightgown had grown, but did not seem life-threatening. Farley laid down beside her and put his arm across her body. Although Leona was only semi-conscious, she moved slightly in the direction of her husband.

Sadie was lapping up some of the boy's blood. I felt as though I would vomit, but didn't. The metallic taste and the increased flow of saliva in my mouth didn't go away.

Connor holstered the gun and reached into a pocket. He held his hand out and I saw that he held a key. He nodded in the direction of Alex's body, and I knew instantly that he was asking me if he should remove the cuffs.es

"Yes," I said, knowing that Connor and I would, by this action, be complicit in saving Farley from the charge of deliberate and perhaps unspeakable homicide.

We're in this together now. We're tied, not just to each other, but to Farley as well.

Into this grisly scene, two Lost Pines police officers, looking terribly young and then, terribly shocked, entered with their own big black guns drawn.

Connor, thank God, was in uniform. He was deliberately staying away from the body of Alex Sterling and, perhaps instinctively, I had moved back too.

The Lost Pines police looked at each other. They'd lowered their guns, but hadn't holstered them. "I'm with the Potts force," Connor said. "I can tell you everything that happened here."

When Connor said that, a lot of the tension seemed to leave the room. Just then, medical personnel arrived, wheeling in a long yellow stretcher. "Check out the woman over there," Connor instructed. Farley, kneeling beside Leona, turned to acknowledge the EMTs, stood, and backed away so they could access his poor wife.

Farley held his hands out and examined them and I remembered that he had done that at the first crime scene, when he had beaten Brandon to death.

One of the young cops spoke into the mic on his shoulder, while the other suggested that we all move into another room. The first cop gestured at us. "Who is the shooter?" he asked.

Connor nodded in the direction of Farley. A flash of surprise appeared on the young cop's face, but then disappeared.

"I think they both should go to the hospital," Connor suggested, as if answering the young cop's unspoken question.

"Careful where you step," someone in the other room said. "And could someone get that dog, please? We've got forensics on the way."

I ran to Sadie's leash on its hook by the front door and handed it to a woman in scrubs. She handed Sadie back to me after she'd attached the leash to Sadie's collar. Sadie's muzzle was pink from the boy's blood.

I held Sadie anyway and saw that her front paws had blood on them too. I sat in a chair and began wiping Sadie with the hem of my dress. If I'd thought about this, I would have been grossed out, but thinking didn't seem to play much of a role in all that had happened since we entered Farley and Leona's home.

The cop in the room with us—I couldn't read his nametag—pulled out a small black object. "I'll be recording this," he said. "Let's start with your name."

His next question was, "And do you know the name of the deceased?"

When I said, "Alex Sterling," the cop's mouth fell open. "Wasn't that other kid named Sterling? The kid last week?" he asked.

"Yes, Brandon Sterling," I said.

"And wait a minute," the cop went on. "That old man. Wasn't he the one who killed that kid, too?"

"Yes," I admitted, looking at Connor and hoping he'd heard.

Connor came close to my chair and squatted down beside it. He spoke as though he'd practiced what he'd begun to say. That Brandon, who was from Potts, had tried to rob Farley and Farley had retaliated by striking the boy with his cane, killing him. "That's the murder you were just talking about." Connor pointed at me. "Eleanor, over there, was a witness."

I nodded, yes.

"Brandon's twin brother, Alex," Connor continued, "came here for revenge. He was planning to avenge his brother's death by harming Farley and his wife."

It sounded so simple without the mindreading aspect to clutter it up! I breathed a lot easier. It made sense.

Connor and I both knew that no one would believe the real story, Farley's clairvoyance and all.

Then the cop asked, "How did you two get involved?"

Connor didn't bat an eye. "We were driving past and saw the lights and heard Leona scream." I watched the cop, thinking, *Please don't ask why we were out in the middle of the night. Please.*

The cop pointed at me and then back at Connor. "Are you two, you know, boyfriend and girlfriend?"

"Yes," Connor said, looking at me, so I said yes, too.

It turned out that Connor and I had to go to the Lost Pines police station and give statements. Connor said he knew Alex's parents and would notify them of their son's loss, but the Lost Pines cop said he'd have to wait and see what his captain had to say about that.

Connor explained being in Lost Pines because Janice Sterling had told him Alex had stolen her car. His immediate suspicion had been that the boy planned revenge.

The cop was wagging his head in agreement, but then he pointed at me, questioning my involvement.

"That's right," Connor said. "I picked Nora—Eleanor—up because I didn't know where Farley lived."

The cop smiled. Another loose end tied up.

Wow! What a fabulous liar Connor is! I thought. I felt no judgement and no shame. I had crossed some barrier, leaving legality and morality behind me.

But then the police separated Connor and me and I was questioned by a man in plain clothes. He identified himself as Detective Smiley, and he did smile quite often. The only time he seemed stern was when he questioned me about the gun.

"Did you give the gun to Farley?" he asked me more than once.

"No."

"Where did Farley get the gun?"

"I don't know. I must have put it down at some point." We'd been over this so often that I felt like demanding a hypnotist who could take me through the sequence of events. "I don't remember. There was so much going on."

I think I put the gun down when I picked the dog up. But when had I done that? Hadn't a police officer handed Sadie to me? But that would have been after the police arrived. I heard my voice getting whinier and whinier. "I don't remember. I remember Connor putting the gun in his holster, but I am not sure when that was. Probably after everything was over." It seemed unfair to me that the cops expected my memory to be crystal clear, what with Alex having been shot and all.

Connor's session had evidently ended before mine. He was in the waiting room looking incredibly crisp.

"They kept asking about the gun," I told him. "They were hung up on how Farley got hold of it."

"I know," Connor said, looking a bit concerned.

CHAPTER SEVENTEEN

It was nearly ten in the morning when Connor and I were able to leave. We exited the Lost Pines station just as Janice and Ray Sterling drove up. "Don't let them see us," I squealed and the two of us hid behind another car to avoid them. Lost Pines law enforcement insisted that they, not Connor, should do the notification.

When Alex's mom and stepdad were safely inside the station, Connor and I all but ran toward his vehicle. I had Sadie on her leash and I felt like a school kid again and surprised myself by laughing.

"There are a couple of things," I said. "There's Brandon's cell phone, remember? Where we clearly see him murdering Brandon."

"You mean this?" Connor produced a phone encased in black leather with a skull imprinted on it.

"You're kidding!"

"It was on the kitchen counter," Connor said. "What else?"

"I don't know, but there's probably something. I watch a lot of crime shows," I said.

"Oh? I thought you watched HGTV."

"I do. But I watch *Law and Order* reruns too."

"Well let's get some breakfast and talk about what we might have missed."

"I can't go looking like this," I said. I was still wearing the crinkle dress, but it had dried blood on it from Sadie. "I have Boost at my house. And I, at least, have to shower, remember?" Plus, we had the dog.

"I do need a Boost," Connor laughed.

All the way home I was inwardly happy that the two of us could laugh again. Who would have imagined laughter coming after all that we'd been through less than twenty-four hours before? Still, I figured there would be a trial, and that would mean the two of us would have to lie under oath. Surely that would be hard for both of us. Weren't we both good people? Good people tell the truth. In a courtroom, especially.

When I told Connor that, he disagreed. "I don't think they'll charge Farley," he said. "Number one, he's ancient, and number two, we bore witness that this was in defense of Leona. At least at the beginning. We saw Alex torturing Leona."

But the actual shooting. We both knew there was no way that could be defended. But above all, it seemed to me it would be suspicious that one old man killed two boys who were twins just a few days apart from each other. Wouldn't that defy explanation?

"Look, it happened," Connor said. "Do you think all of Farley's visions would make things easier or harder to believe? And don't forget, you would have to tell them about the phone. About how you picked it up and kept it. I think we ought to let sleeping dogs lie."

Sleeping dogs. But Connor was the cop, so he should know.

"After we clean up," Connor said, "I think we should go get your car. That's a big loose end."

"Poor Slick," I said, and before Connor could say anything I shouted, "Yes, I named my car. So what?"

Connor laughed. "My truck has a name, too. My buddies at the station call it, 'The Green Heap.' And sometimes they are more formal and call it 'The Classic Green Heap.'

I grew serious again. "Do you think the clerk at that convenience store will blow the whistle?"

"Well, that's why we need to get your car. We don't want anyone talking to that clerk. On the off chance he remembers anything, which I doubt."

"You could have been a criminal," I said, admiring his facility with invention.

"That's why I'm a good cop," Connor said. "But after all these lies," he admitted, "I think I'll have to resign."

We went down the highway toward Potts and sure enough, there was Slick, right where I'd left the car.

"Amazing," Connor said, "that nobody tried to steal it. Of course, this place is open twenty-four hours a day," meaning the convenience store. He parked beside my car.

"I don't think you should take Sadie in there," he said, "but I'm going to buy some dog food. We don't know how long we'll have this pup."

We both got out of the car, Connor headed toward the store, and Sadie and I checked my car out. Connor had handed me something, a little black zip up container, but I hadn't opened it yet.

When I opened the passenger door, Sadie hopped in the way she had the day of the first murder. "Good girl," I said, as though that action formed a sort of parenthesis around the whole incident.

Connor came out with a bag. I closed Sadie into the car. "Did you start it?" he asked me.

"That was the problem," I said, "remember?"

"Did you open that case I gave you?"

"No," I had to admit. In fact, I'd put it inside the car with Sadie.

Connor opened the car door and pulled the zip case out. He

made a show of it, like a magician. "Welcome to the modern world, Miss Armitage. With this device, I will start your car. Like magic."

The thing inside did have those red and black clip on things that jumper cables had, only a teeny version. "Open the hood," he told me, and he attached the clips to the battery. "Now get in and turn the key," he said.

I thought he was crazy, but got in, turned the key, and Slick's engine roared. I powered the window down. "What is that thing?" I asked. "Is it something only police have?"

"Here," Connor disconnected it and zipped it back up. "Take it just in case," Connor said. "I have to get rid of this cruiser. I'll get my truck and come back. Will you be all right by yourself?"

Ordinarily I would have argued that I've always been all right by myself, but I didn't feel angry; I felt not a twinge of my customary response. "I'm not by myself," I teased. "I have a dog."

"Okay," Connor agreed. "See you in a couple of hours."

When Connor returned, I was sitting on the sofa with the contents of Farley's briefcase spread out in front of me. Sadie padded around the house, investigating, but she never came near the clippings and photos on the coffee table.

That thing about Farley seeing into the future of those kids he called *certain children* wasn't as hard to believe as the twin thing. Assuming that Farley had read Brandon's mind, was there anything that said Alex's thoughts could have been there, in the wrong twin's head? Maybe I should call Doctor Menard again, now that I knew Alex and Brandon had been conjoined. But, actually, I probably shouldn't, because that would mean I would be talking about the part of this Farley thing that Connor and I had resolved to keep secret.

I had appeared crazy enough to the outside world. No need to compound it.

When he got back to my house, Connor obviously had been thinking about the clairvoyance angle too. But he began by admonishing me. "That Great Silkie story is nothing like the Quaker Oats box and it's nothing like our story, the Farley thing."

"Huh?"

"The Great Silkie. He impregnates a woman and goes back to the sea, and then the woman gives birth to a hunter who ends up killing him."

"But the silkie predicts that it's going to happen!" I insisted.

"Whatever you say. And for that matter, it isn't like the Quaker Oats box either."

"Do we have to go through this now?" I asked.

"Not this. Not right this minute," he allowed. "But at some point, I would really like to know what made you believe Farley was clairvoyant. You are not a gullible person."

I led him over to the coffee table where I had the contents of Farley's briefcase spread out.

"Here's this boy, Larry Olsen," I grabbed a magazine article about Larry all grown up. He was a famous defense lawyer. "Farley took a look at him in the playground when Larry was a young kid and, bam, he saw him in his adult life presenting a case to a jury."

"Farley says."

"No, he knew. He told me that he knew. And here's Audrey Standish," I pulled another article out. "He saw her as a ballerina back when she was just a skinny kid."

"Farley says," Connor repeated. Connor said it sounded like a lot of hooey and went on to dismiss the stuff in Farley's briefcase. Farley had pictures of kids and then a picture of the kid all grown up, but the fact that Farley had predicted what would happen to the kid was never proven.

"Don't you get it?" Connor insisted. "Farley said he knew how they'd grow up, what they'd be, who they married, but so what? There's no proof that he really did know those things. He already had seen how these children turned out, so all he had to say was that he knew it all along. So maybe you and Leona believed him, but there's no way any sane person would. Not that you and Leona aren't sane," he added.

He wouldn't let it go. "There's no way of proving Farley could see the future. Why would you think he was telling the truth?"

"Leona believed him. And she seemed kind of proud of him because of it. I remember her smile when I saw her for the first time and she used that phrase, *certain children*."

"Certain children. Big deal."

"Okay," I said. "How about this: Farley could see the past, too."

"Oh, boy."

"He knew my parents called me Button."

"Right. But you probably mentioned it or something. Why did they call you that, by the way? Or should I ask Farley."

I punched his arm, a teeny punch, not a real one.

"No. The Button thing was something I never talked about because it reminded me that my parents were gone." I didn't like thinking about that. My mother had fallen ill, but my dad's death had happened suddenly, not long after.

I pushed the memory away. "Oh, listen, Connor, Farley knew a lot more. He knew everything. There's no way I would have doubted him."

"Tell me what he knew," Connor said, his voice soft. I couldn't help thinking about the show, *Law & Order Special Victims Unit*, where Olivia Benson talked to rape victims. I could tell by the way he was talking that he knew I was holding something important from him.

I looked into Connor's eyes and decided to take a chance.

"I will tell you, Connor, but you have to promise not to laugh or interrupt or tell anybody. I would hate you if you did."

"I won't do either of those things."

"And," I continued, "you have to promise not to act as though I haven't told you something important. Because this is very important to me. This completely shaped my life."

"I promise."

I swallowed and said, "Okay. I'm forty-nine years old, Connor, and I've had sex exactly once. Once, when I was sixteen. Farley knew about that and he knew about why."

I heard myself going through the whole story about my date with Louis Figulski, even telling him what I was wearing. I kept going, admitting how I'd wanted to make out with Louis, even wanted to have sex with him. But then I got to the part about Louis not being able to finish and slapping me and saying that something had to be wrong with me. I told him about Louis just before he took me home, saying my vagina was too big. I was sniveling by this time, gulping out the words. "And he didn't say it like that, Connor. I won't even tell you the words he used, but that was it for me. I never had sex again. I never wanted to have sex again. I knew no one would find sex with me pleasurable, and I just sort of didn't want to."

"Did you ever talk to a doctor about it?" he asked.

"I talked to my gynecologist and she said I was normal."

"And so?"

"It didn't help. I didn't really believe her."

Connor sighed audibly. "Stop," he said. "You tend to interpret things in the worst possible way. That's what you do. About pretty much everything. But listen, I want you to think about another way of interpreting the Louis Figulski experience, okay? The interpretation that makes more sense to me than the one you've been carrying around. Okay?"

I wiped snot away with my knuckle and dropped my head. Connor put a finger under my chin and lifted it. "Look at me," he instructed. "Come on. Look at me."

I did.

"There's another explanation, and that is, that Louis Figulski..."

I put my hands over my ears the way a kid would. I was shaking my head, no, no, no. I was afraid. I didn't know what he might say. I didn't want to hear what he thought. I was ashamed that I'd even told him. I was ashamed that Farley knew. I was so ashamed. Ashamed about all of it. Ashamed about my body and the cavern that was my vagina. The cavern that doomed me.

"I'm a mess, Connor, please let's stop talking about it." I stood up, feeling panicky. Didn't Connor realize I just wanted to let the whole thing drop, never talk about it, never think about it. Maybe I should never see Officer Connor Randall ever, ever again.

But he grabbed me and he pulled me back down beside him. He hung on to my wrist. I knew I couldn't get away. *The minute this conversation is over, I'm gone*, I thought, steeling myself.

"Chances are," Connor said, forming his words slowly and deliberately, "that Louis Fucking Figulski had the smallest pecker in America. The smallest pecker on the planet. So of course you felt big to him. He had a teeny little dick. Louis Figulski had a pint-sized prick and he would have been dissatisfied no matter who the woman was.

"Let's Google Louis Figulski," Connor went on. "Let's see what he's up to. Maybe he's in some carnival somewhere, World's Smallest Penis."

I started laughing hysterically. It was like the 4711 moment the night I'd met him. The surprise of it. The way it served as an antidote to the way I had of closing myself up, of warding everyone away.

Somehow Connor moved me to his side and pressed against me, holding me tight. I pulled my legs up onto the sofa and wriggled toward him. I was still laughing, but as my laughter faded, I felt a softening inside. I felt pleasure that I'd met someone who could know this awful thing about me and make me laugh about it. I felt pleasure feeling the warmth of Connor's body, but especially, feeling the safety of it.

Connor kissed me, not passionately, but sweetly. "We'll be fine," he said, "You and me. We'll be fine. It may take a while, but I think it's worth trying."

I felt a flash of happiness but said nothing.

Connor was undaunted. "Look," he said. "I feel good when I'm with you. Something about it feels right. That night you called me... I can't tell you how happy I was to hear your voice."

The space between my eyes pinched, which it always does when I'm about to cry.

"I don't have any faith in this working out," I said, with sobs punctuating my words.

Connor touched my face. "I think I have enough faith for both of us," he told me.

CHAPTER EIGHTEEN

JANUARY 3, 2020

We walked Sadie together and we laughed at some of her antics. We didn't go to the Riverwalk, but went up my driveway to the road, which looped around a subdivision in a three-mile circle.

We also drove past Farley and Leona's house every day, hoping to see a sign of life. It wasn't long before we noticed the wooden door open and the aluminum storm door the only barrier to entry. I stayed in the truck while Connor walked up to the door and knocked. Leona was smiling at him, inviting him in.

He waved to me to come in and of course I brought Sadie. The dog was ecstatic. She leapt straight up, turned herself around, landed and did it again. We were all surprised by her athleticism.

Leona seemed happy to see her.

Leona moved stiffly, and I realized her injuries were causing her considerable pain. "Farley is napping," she told us, removing Sadie's leash and hanging it on the hook near the door. Sadie left the room. "She wants her foot," Leona told us.

The foot. I remembered the foot. I had been revolted by it, but now it seemed quite tame.

"We are so grateful to you both," she said.

I wondered what Farley had told Leona about the murders, but there was no way I would ever bring that up. Even if he'd told his wife, I doubted she'd want to talk about it. I searched her face, thinking I'd see signs of what she knew there, but saw nothing except a pleasant older woman happy to see us and her dog again.

"I can make coffee," Leona offered.

Connor and I said 'no' together.

"Let's sit then," she led us into the kitchen.

"We can't stay," Connor said.

"I'm sorry," I added.

"Thank you for taking care of Sadie," she told me. She extended a slender hand and I took it, pressed it slightly. I could see stitches on her neck when I stood on this side of her.

The thought of being stabbed with a corkscrew. With a corkscrew! Although Connor defended his choice, saying it indicated that Alex had acted spontaneously, without pre-planning his attack.

"Would you like me to awaken Farley?" she asked.

"Oh, no," I said, and exchanged a glance with Connor.

I gave their home—as much as I could see of it—a quick once over. It held a sadness, a feeling of time standing still. There were still signs of disruption here and there.

Leona saw me evaluating her surroundings. "We'll be working on it soon. Spiffing it up a bit."

I was embarrassed. But when Connor and I stepped outside, I noticed that the mailbox was no longer surrounded by junk mail. That was a good start.

. . .

Connor and I did not immediately have sex. Connor didn't even try, though he would kiss me, at first briefly and then at greater length. I looked forward to his kisses, and yes, I felt a stirring between my legs, a kind of need to feel even closer to him than he and I had been. We always ended it there, both of us fully clothed.

It seemed silly at age forty-nine to be thinking about going *all the way*. But just that morning, I knew where things were headed. I was walking behind Connor, and I watched the way his back muscles moved and what a good-looking hind end he had. I imagined running my hands over those, and under his clothes, too. In teen-aged parlance, I was horny!

And then, one afternoon, I led him to my bed and it was I who made every advance, turning my face toward his, moving my hand along his shoulder, his chest, along his thigh. I could hear my own breathing, fast and thick, and that alone emboldened me.

I took the time to look at him. His eyes were closed, but lightly. Perhaps he thought he was dreaming. Meanwhile, I rubbed my cheeks, my lips against the bristle of the hair on his body.

What I felt was wonder. Had you asked me, "What would you do if...?" I would have had no answer, but with Connor, I knew, my body knew, my hands, my tongue knew. I was certain and alive.

When he spoke, he said, "You feel so good," and what occurred to me was, yes, lovemaking is that simple. It had always been simple. But I was glad I had waited for Connor. Glad to have him and be had by him. When he put his arms around me, and I put mine around him, I knew I was where I had long belonged.

Connor was correct about the way things eventually turned out for Farley. Unexpectedly, the Potts police were livid that Connor's gun had been used to kill Alex, even if Farley had used it to defend his wife. The Lost Pines police still had the gun, in fact, and that made things worse. A lot of bureaucratic paperwork was involved in its return and even the mayor of Potts got involved.

Connor's five fellow officers were mad at their bosses because of the hard time they were giving Connor. They even threatened to go out on strike, but Connor told them it was all right and kept that from happening.

In the end, all of the squabbling about Connor's gun—Glock this and Glock that—turned out to be a blessing, really, because it made Connor's resignation plausible, whereas, otherwise, Connor's leaving the Potts police force might have seemed kind of suspicious.

But that meant Connor was unemployed.

CHAPTER NINETEEN

MARCH 19, 2020

Connor came in with a big, satisfied smile. "One of my old buddies in Potts gave me a heads up about someone trying to get in touch with me. A producer. I'm supposed to call him back."

"Oh my God. Does that mean they know the whole story? The real story?"

"I don't think so, but I'll call him tomorrow and we'll see what's up."

What was up was, the television show, *Crimebeat,* had somehow heard that a retired science teacher in his 70s here in Texas had killed twins several days apart And in both cases, it was self-defense. The teacher hadn't been prosecuted. *Crimebeat* was writing a script about it, and they wanted Connor to be a consultant. For real money!

"Imagine if they knew the real story. About Farley's visions," I said.

"Don't even think about it. Because you and I and Farley, too, would be in real trouble if anyone knew. We'll have to coach Farley so he doesn't say anything."

We didn't know what Leona knew. We decided it was unlikely that Farley had told her the complete story.

APRIL 2, 2020

We asked Farley and Leona to come to my place. The four of us sat by the river and we built a fire in the pit and sat upwind of it. It was pleasant. I wore a blue cotton lightweight dress that looked like something a 1940s housewife might wear. Leona looked youthful in jeans and a tee shirt. Farley had his customary white shirt and red bowtie. Sadie ran around looking for bugs and lizards. Connor told the couple about the interest on the part of the television people.

It turned out Farley and Leona already knew. Farley said he would not consent to an interview, nor would Leona. "We don't want to rehash all that," he said. "It's bad enough that it happened, but why make it worse by telling everybody in the world?"

"It's public information," Connor said. "They can cover the story, but they'll have to do it without interviewing you."

"Or Leona," Farley insisted. He looked over at his wife, but she hadn't reacted to hearing her name. Farley changed the subject. "Which reminds me, Eleanor, you still have my briefcase."

I froze. I did have it and if I kept it, I could be sure the clairvoyant aspect of the murders would not come out.

It must have shown fear on my face, because Farley sought to assuage me. "I think we ought to burn it all," Farley said. "All the pictures, the clippings. Let the whole thing go up in smoke."

"Right now," Connor said. He ran up to the house and brought the briefcase down. It was as if he wanted to make certain Farley got rid of the stuff before he could change his mind.

Farley and Connor and I took turns tossing the photos and newspaper articles into the fire. Leona sat silent.

We heard Sadie, in the distance, barking ferociously. Leona stood and dusted herself. "I'll go," she said. "It sounds like her possum bark." We three watched as she took Farley's new cane and went off in search of the dog.

Once she was out of earshot, Farley said, "And now this," holding up a little black something. "It's the SIM card from the boy's phone."

We also burned the SIM card and threw its melted remains as well as the phone and the leather case out into the river.

Connor told Farley that he'd signed on as a consultant on the *Crimebeat* project, but Farley was okay with that.

Farley didn't know I had Brandon Sterling's selfie—the first murder—on my computer. Later I asked Connor if I should delete it.

"Deleting stuff is a waste of time. Just don't give anyone any reason to go to your computer. In fact, let's go to Electrix and get you a new one and put the old one away somewhere."

I thought of the four old computers I had stashed away in the room where I kept my textiles. I'd put the computers in there when something had gone wrong with them. I had everything from an old Dell to a couple of Macs. I couldn't even recall why the Macs had been abandoned. It was probably my designer's idea. Technically, they all belonged to her, but I doubted she'd be asking for them.

"This is a beautiful place," Farley said, looking up the slope to my home. "I'm thinking that I may have to start spiffing up our house a bit. Get rid of the weeds, maybe plant some petunias."

I smiled. Leona and Farley had used the same expression, "spiffing up," when talking about their home.

Leona approached with a wriggling Sadie, and Farley stood and dropped the dog's collar and leash over Sadie's head.

"A possum may sound harmless," Farley said, "but under pressure, they are fierce." We all nodded. I don't know about Connor or Leona, but I was thinking of Farley and the pressure of his clairvoyance.

I didn't think of it often. I knew that Connor and I, in the eyes of jurisprudence, had helped to cover up a serious crime. In its mere outline, the murders were sensational enough for television. I could only imagine what it would be like if the full facts were known.

MAY 3, 2020

It was a while before I wanted to walk on the Riverwalk again, but eventually I did. There were things about it that I wanted to share with Connor. That particular morning, I was babbling about the ducks and we were very near the spot where the bold female duck I admired had wandered through the long pipe to lay her eggs.

I told Connor how inspiring I'd found it. "Now she's gone. She had her ducklings and she's back in the world again."

"Reminds me of someone I know," he said.

I was taken aback. I had not realized how true that was until just that moment. "Quack," I said. "Quack quack quack."

He pulled me close and we both laughed. We sat on a green metal bench and eventually, Carl came along.

"Hey," he said to Connor. "Is that Syclone pickup in the parking lot yours?"

"Yessir," Connor told him.

"You thinking of restoring it?" Carl asked.

Connor laughed. "One day, sure."

"You ever get to where you want a really fine paint job, you call me." He fished in his pocket and handed Connor a business card. Then, without warning, he sat down on the bench beside me.

He gestured at me. "Your wife ever tell you how she got those cops to give me back my phone?"

Connor and I weren't married, but neither of us said anything about Carl's assumption.

"Yep," Carl went on, "Them cops probably would have kept it if it hadn't been for Eleanor here."

I smiled. I didn't think it was true, but for some reason, Carl had been reluctant to approach the police without me by his side.

"Hard to do body business without a cell phone, don't you know. I got the best examples of my work right here, lots of pictures, ready to go." He held the camo-covered phone aloft. "Let me show you a couple," he tapped a few buttons and then handed the phone across me to Connor. "They say candy-apple red is dead, but I painted this one just about a month ago and it looks pretty alive to me."

Connor admired it and handed the phone back. "You do good work, Carl."

"And here's a special color I whipped up for an old Corvette." He handed the phone across again.

"Nice," Connor said, drawing the word out to indicate he really did admire it. "Even Shorty would think so."

Shorty? But Carl seemed to know him too. "Thanks," he said.

Connor tried to include me, saying Shorty was someone from *Iron Resurrection*, but that didn't clarify anything.

"I do my own body work, too," Carl said, "but your truck looks pretty straight to me." Carl tapped some more buttons and showed us an SUV with a pretty much mangled front end. "You know that Farron fellow? He's a big shot. Sits on the council?"

I perked up at that. "Ronald Farron?"

"Yeah. This is what he came in with right after he hit a deer." He held the phone so that Connor and I could both see it. "And this here's After. I fixed that up like it never even happened. Had to do it fast and on the QT because he didn't want his wife to find out."

I reached for Connor's hand and squeezed it. "When was this, Carl?" Connor asked, his voice calm and steady.

"It was Fourth of July," Carl said. "This coming Fourth will be two years. I was closed, but he came by the house, banging on my door."

I squeezed Connor's fingers even tighter. It seemed possible that the deer Ronald Farron had hit was my friend, Megan McCann. Or was I crazy?

Connor broke free of my grasp and pulled a folded piece of paper out of his pocket and, eventually, a stub of pencil. "Carl? I'd like you to email those pictures to me, all right? Here's my address."

"Sure thing," Carl said.

"Not just the paint job," Connor emphasized, "but the body work too."

"Will do." Carl stood up and pocketed his cell phone and what Connor had written. "I got more on my computer," Carl said. "I document all the work, stage by stage."

"Connor," I said, when Carl was out of earshot. "Do you think there's a chance that slimy bastard... oh, I can't even say it."

"A good chance," Connor said. "But slow down, Button. Let's see how this plays out."

CHAPTER TWENTY

JUNE 12, 2020

I couldn't believe it when I suggested Connor rent out his place in Potts as an Air Bnb and stay with me. It would mean additional income for him and we could spend more time together, I explained. Not that the *Crimebeat* thing wouldn't be rewarding him nicely.

"Potts doesn't get a lot of tourists," Connor said. But before I could think he was just inventing an excuse not to be with me, he added, "I think I'll just sell my place outright. But living with your décor, Button, I just don't know."

"Maria Shriver and Arnold Schwarzenegger made it work. At least while they were together. I saw a show about their house."

"Spare me," Connor said, though his voice said he was teasing.

I wanted to tell him how much I loved the things we were learning about each other and the way he brought to light how odd some of my own choices seemed. When he found out, for instance, that I bought Dove bath soap for men, for example. And how huffy I got explaining that I needed something strong after I'd gardened.

I found out that he spent nearly every day jogging, except that he insisted it was called 'running,' not 'jogging.' My god, he'd erected a chin bar on the back patio!

"Well," I said. "At least I know you won't be hanging a picture of those dogs playing poker."

"How about *The Last Supper*?" he asked. "Could I hang that?"

"Only if it's the original Leonardo de Vinci," I told him. "But of course that's a huge mural." Then I heard myself saying, "You know what? Let's go to Italy and see the original."

"I don't even have a passport," Connor said. "I'm just a country boy. Of course, I did see on the Internet that the place where they make that 4711 stuff you like so much gives tours."

"Oh my God!" I screamed, laughing crazily. But somehow, we both realized that one day soon we just might go.

JUNE 18, 2020

Connor had been sent DVDs of *Crimebeat* so that he could get an idea of what the show was like. They were half-hour episodes done in black and white. They featured real pictures of crime scenes. I watched two of them and found them enormously depressing. It wasn't only the look of the show; it was also that ordinary people turned out to be the murderers. In both of them, the victims were women whose marriages seemed to be perfect. Then police found out the husbands were having affairs, one with an office mate and the other with the woman who lived next door. Evil and duplicity, betrayal. And ugliness. Their surroundings. The bloodstains.

"I can't watch these," I told Connor. "They are too depressing."

"It's okay. You don't have to. In fact, I can watch them somewhere else. I can go to another room and watch them on my computer."

"Please." I felt stupid. I did watch *Law & Order*, and I had seen actual murders. What was wrong with me? "I feel foolish," I admitted. I was reminded, though I didn't share it, of the way I'd felt in high school art class, when the student beside me was always painting drab scenes that I was afraid I'd be drawn into.

Did it mean I was hopelessly superficial?

Connor walked past me with his laptop. "Any special place you want me to go?" he asked.

"The bedroom?" I suggested. Then I asked, "How many? How many more do you have to see?"

"Nobody said, but they sent a lot of them."

"It seems weird that a television show would be interested in this without knowing the whole story. The clairvoyance stuff, I mean."

"Staid retired science teacher kills two teenage boys, days apart, who are twins? It's interesting even if you don't know the rest. And please stop talking about the rest. Don't even think about it."

I retreated to my studio and googled a site that never failed to cheer me. It was a virtual catalog of wallpaper for rooms for children. After looking at chickens and ducks and fairies and whales, I always felt better.

What did Brandon and Alex have on their walls?

Meanwhile, I had a specific project to complete. Leona's 80th birthday was coming up and Farley had given me a plastic bag full of his old ties. From these, I was to use various combinations to make a small purse for Leona, a gift from her husband. I thought it was a sweet idea. Farley had offered to pay me to do it, but of course I demurred.

I had the ties arrayed on a shelf, the widest parts hanging over the edge. It was easy to see what would go with what. I was especially interested in the patterned ties. There were so many, and each was so different from the other.

I had already drawn a pattern, a simple fold over top with cord that tied over a button. The button was one I'd purchased three years earlier. It was ivory, with a dragon painted on the face of it. I wouldn't tell Leona or Farley or even Connor how valuable it was. I would just add it as my contribution, the perfect touch to compliment the fabric choice.

But of course, the dragon would govern the selection of cloth. Nothing wimpy. Strong colors and patterns.

A long time passed before I sat at the sewing machine. And just then Connor appeared.

"I watched as many as I want to watch," he said. "And you were right, they're depressing. But this," he said, pointing at the ties I'd cut, "is anything but."

"Thanks," I said. "I wanted it to be bold, but at the same time, uplifting." I realized I didn't know if Connor owned any ties or even a suit. And it didn't matter. Proximity to murder had changed me.

"When is Leona's birthday party?"

"Saturday."

"Uh, I'm sorry to tell you this, sweetie, but the producer and the scriptwriter are coming into town Friday evening. On Saturday I am driving them around Lost Pines and then taking them to Potts."

"It isn't until three," I tried.

"I'll probably be tied up the whole day," he said.

I shrugged. So, it goes.

I had wrapped Leona's bag in lavender tissue and tied it with cord. I handed it to Farley surreptitiously. I tried to notice the way Leona moved. She'd suffered a number of puncture wounds in various places. Was she in pain?

She really looked her age, too, but a lot of it was due to the way she wore her hair and the dowdy clothes she wore, including a bulky and baggy cardigan. In addition, her face had deep creases and her lips seemed to be turning inward, disappearing.

Although I'd met her for the first time not terribly long ago, she seemed to have aged considerably since then. Still, when Farley handed her the package and she saw the bag inside, her mouth opened in surprise and then an enormous smile beat back the years. "Farley," she said, butting his shoulder with her head. "And Nora, is this your handiwork?"

"I did have something to do with it," I said. "But the fabrics! Farley, tell her about the fabrics."

Farley pointed at various pieces, identifying his ties. Leona was delighted. "But the button," she said. "It's so..." she stopped, not having found the proper word. She rubbed her finger over the worn surface and said, "Special. It's so very special." Suddenly she stood up. "I have to do this justice," she said. "I'll be back." She moved with an energy I hadn't seen before and left the room.

"Come into the kitchen," Farley said. "I'll make us some tea."

I followed him and sat at the kitchen table. It was cluttered with gloves and bills and coins. Farley filled a whistling tea kettle as I moved some of the items away so that he'd have a place to put a cup and saucer in front of me.

That was when I gasped. The sound was sufficiently loud for Farley to turn, the kettle in hand. I tried to explain. I'd gasped because I'd uncovered a Lost Pines newspaper with a picture of Ronald Farron smack on the front page. The headline said that he'd said he was planning to run for U.S. Congress when it was time to file.

"I just can't believe this," I told Farley. "People say our government is corrupt and then we have people like this..." I didn't know how to finish. It was as if a film whirred through my mind. Farron's car slamming into Megan, backing away, him driving off and talking Carl into getting rid of the evidence.

When I looked up again, Farley was staring at me, his head cocked.

"I'm sorry," I mumbled.

"No, Button," he said. "I promise you, it will end." With that, he took the kettle he had been holding and held it an inch over Farron's chubby-cheeked image. "Look," he said, and let the kettle fall onto it. The bottom of the kettle covered the photograph and the headline as well.

I laughed just as Leona swept into the room.

She was wearing a sarong, turquoise and white. Over one shoulder she'd draped a multicolored shawl. It was flowered at the base. Above that were some bright gold designs that looked like a row of suns. Another layer was above that, red, black and gold stripes. It was clearly ethnic in origin.

She'd put the bag I'd made over one shoulder and it held its own, even among the sea of pattern and color that she'd chosen. She turned in a tight circle, her arms outstretched. She had loosened her hair, and it lifted and swirled with her. The fabric did as well, a wonderful draped effect.

"My darling Leona," Farley said, rising and taking her into his arms.

"Wait," Leona said, pulling off her shoes.

They began to dance to a tune that Farley, at first was humming. Then Leona joined in. Farley buried his fingers into her hair.

I got up to leave, aware that they were now oblivious to my presence. Avoiding any contact with them, I picked up Leona's shoes and placed them on the kitchen table lest the two step on one and stumble.

When I got outside and into my car, I marveled at what I'd seen. When they were dancing, they both seemed younger than their years. I thought about the shawl. Had they been hippies? I wondered.

I could barely wait to tell Connor.

. . .

It was maybe five in the evening when Connor, accompanied by two striking women, arrived.

Connor introduced me to Sheena, the executive producer, and Diane, the writer. Diane was wearing blue jeans, but Sheena was wearing raw silk, a chemise.

"Connor told us the two of you met because of the first murder," Sheena said brightly. "If our show was longer, we could do a coda on that. Very cute," she turned to Diane who vigorously shook her head in assent.

Although I smiled along with them, there was nothing I wanted less. I tried to read Connor's expression, but couldn't tell if his laughter was real or feigned, like mine.

Diane addressed me. "I understand you got to know the twins' mother," she said.

Sheena piped up. "If you could get her talking—not on camera, of course, but just generally, that would be divine. Perhaps she'd tell you more about the Siamese element then she would tell Connor or a stranger."

"What does that have to do with it?" I was a bit shocked. Had Connor told them that? Or did they find it out some other way?

Sheena said, "Siamese twins? That's pure gold. It makes the whole story sexier. We were a little bit short on the initial motive, but with the Siamese element, no one will even wonder what the motive was. You know, for—what was his name? Alex. To attack the old man."

"I thought it was robbery," I said. She meant Brandon, not Alex, but I didn't see the point of correcting her.

"Whatever," Sheena said.

"I think I can get some information from Juvenile Justice about both boys," Connor said. "And the Potts police records have more."

"Did you talk to the Sterlings?" I asked.

"No," Connor said. "We just drove by."

"I was quite surprised by their home," Sheena said, "Weren't you, Di?" She didn't wait for an answer. "A lot of the settings for these things are pretty scuzzy."

I remembered the solid brick Craftsman, its wonderful porch. The furnishings inside were impressive, too.

"Anyway," Sheena said, "Connor is going to give Diane the backstory. It helps that she's been here, of course."

"What exactly will happen?" I asked. "After there's a script. Will there actually be cameras here?"

"Just to do some shots where things happened. The Sterling house, the Clements house, the path along the river. Maybe three days max, very low key. Then some interviews. We need permissions for those. One from you, by the way."

"What if people don't want to be interviewed?" I remembered that Farley didn't. Probably Leona wouldn't want that either.

"Re-creations," Diane said.

"They're like little movies," Sheena explained. "Actors, set, very realistic. Anyway, we've got to go. We have the 11 p.m. flight back to New York. I think it's the last one."

Connor stood up, so I did too.

"Connor will have to come to New York at some point," Sheena said to me. "Why not come with? After the business part, you and I could go shopping."

"Sounds like a plan," I said.

Connor and I were in the doorway waving as they drove off in their rental car. "I bet you wanted to deck her," Connor said.

"Who?"

"Sheena. When she made that dig about taking you shopping."

"That was a compliment!" I said. "She was wearing Armani," I continued. "And did you see her bag? It was Hermes, probably a couple thousand dollars! She was telling me she admired my taste."

"How did she know a thing about your taste?"

"I don't want to tell you," I said. "But I will. She knew because I'm wearing Alexander McQueen," I said. "Didn't you see the way she looked me over?"

"Okay. Clearly, it's a woman thing."

"I'm sure men do it too." I should have mentioned the way he and Carl had swooned over Connor's ramshackle truck.

"Oh, right," he said, "These pants? Levi Strauss. And the shirt, let's see. Does Wal-Mart have its own brand?"

"That is not a Wal-Mart shirt," I said. "Wal-Mart doesn't use that grade of cotton."

"How do you know it's cotton? Maybe it's polyester."

"It's cotton. And not all polyesters are bad. Come on, Connor, it's my *job*."

I wasn't seriously irked. Especially since I hadn't yet told him about Leona and Farley's romantic interlude. "Let's sit down," I said. "I have a little tale to tell."

There is something wonderful when you tell a person something and he or she gets exactly what you want them to get. I have had that feeling a couple of times in my life. Once I was sitting on the sofa with my father watching a movie. A character drove up in a sports car I'd once talked about driving when I had my driver's license. I was maybe 13 at the time.

When the scene began, my father asked, "Is that it?"

And I knew he meant the car. "That's *it*," I said.

Another time was when my mother and I were about to drive to a fabric store downtown. I reminded her that one of our neighbors had once asked if she could go along. "No," my mother said.

"Why not?" I asked. My mother was usually a generous and outgoing person.

"Because then we'll have to talk," she said.

I knew exactly what she meant, because she and I often drove with the radio loud, and we didn't talk, but we both enjoyed it. "Nora, do you know what I mean?"

"Yes. We'd have to be our social selves instead of being our real selves."

My mother laughed. "That's it exactly."

When people say 'intimacy,' they often mean sexual intimacy, but the incidents I'm describing describe intimacy of another sort. Maybe a deeper sort.

"What was the song they were humming," Connor asked.

"It went," and I replicated the melody.

"*Always,*" he said. "Even Stevie Wonder recorded it."

Later, while he was outlining the various tasks ahead of him for the *Crimebeat* show, I Googled the song. When I read the words, I was much moved.

I'll be loving you always
With a heart that's true always
When the things you planned
Need a helping hand
I will understand always.

Then the melody changed and the words went.

Not for just an hour
Not for just a day
Not for just a year, but always.

CHAPTER TWENTY-ONE

JUNE 12, 2020

I was still in bed when Connor came into the room holding something. It was Sadie. He sat down on the bed and let go of her and she instantly came to start licking my face.

"Where did she come from?" I asked.

"Farley wanted us to watch her. He and Leona were off somewhere overnight. Probably the mood they were in last night has lingered."

"Overnight? You mean tonight?"

"You need some coffee, love," he said.

Sadie followed him when he left the room. An overnight seemed odd, but why shouldn't they go? What was wrong with me? I was thinking about them as though they were children.

I hit the switch that made the back of the bed go up, but made no attempt to get out of it and start the day. Where would they have gone? Had they told Connor? Did either of them have a cell phone so that we could reach them?

Connor came in with a mug. I took it and looked inside. Good.

He remembered that I liked to drink a half-full cup at a time. "You look worried," he said.

"I know. I'm being stupid. But did you see Leona? Was she in the car? Was it that big American car that's always in their driveway."

"I don't know about Leona, but yes, it was that Mercury of theirs. I have to say, I'm surprised the thing started. He left it running when he came to the door." He tousled my hair. "Come on, kid. We have some serious dog-sitting to do."

The coffee made me feel human again. Connor made his coffee in a Chemex pot that looked like something from a chemistry lab. He was very serious about it, even grinding Kona beans that he ordered online. But I had to admit, it was much better than the coffee that my Mr. Bean maker made.

I decided to get another half cup before I got dressed.

Connor was emptying a shopping bag.

"Why all the dog food?" I asked.

"I don't know," he said. He stacked the cans on the counter. There were at least ten. Each was the size of the average tuna can.

"Do you think she's hungry?" I asked.

She sat at Connor's feet, staring intently. "No," he said. "Farley was clear that she had her morning meal and shouldn't eat again until six tonight. He said she could very quickly become overweight, so I was only to feed her half a can in the evening and half a can tomorrow morning. Look, there's even a plastic lid for the can." He held it up.

"And he brought that whole shopping bag of food?" I said.

"I think it's her toys and things," he said.

I went over to the bag and peered, then reached inside. "That stupid foot is here," I said, pulling it out and dropping it in front of the dog. Instead of taking it, she continued looking up at the kitchen counter. "Are you sure they're just going overnight?"

"I'm pretty sure that's what he said."

Farley had also included Sadie's leash and collar and a towel. "Why would Sadie have a towel?"

Connor shrugged.

"There's more," I said, pulling out an envelope that lay flat across the bottom of the bag. It wasn't sealed, so I opened it. "Ha!" I said, "Sadie is registered. Guess how old she is?"

"Thirty," Connor said.

"She's ten. She was born in 2010."

"Do we know the day?"

"February 9. I guess this is Sadie's little travel bag. And that's why all her stuff is in it. Or else," I tried to sound as though I was joking, "Or maybe Farley and Leona have run off. To the Casbah."

We were both quiet for a minute. "Tell me what you're thinking."

"I don't know what I'm thinking," I said. "I just feel, I don't know, odd. Troubled. Suspicious. Something isn't right."

"Let's just wait and see," Connor said. But his brow, like my own, was furrowed.

Later, early afternoon, I saw Sadie in the great room, standing by the door. Maybe Farley had come back, I thought. But then the fur along Sadie's back stood up in a prominent line, and she began to growl.

Connor walked forward with the leash and collar, captured Sadie, and opened the door wide.

Standing there was Juanita Star, the editor of the newspaper. "I'm here to talk to Eleanor," she said. And Connor stepped aside to let her come in. She carried a cassette recorder—an old one, rather large—and some electrical cords. "Let me take that," Connor said, and Juanita took advantage of the opportunity to slip out of her coat. I came forward and took it, introducing her to Connor.

"I didn't know your phone number," Juanita said, "but everyone knows where you live."

"Let's sit down," I said, leading the way to the furniture grouped nearby. We all sat.

"May I record?" Juanita asked.

She had addressed the request to me, but Connor interrupted. "Record what?"

"I've been told that you, Eleanor, and your friend Connor here, were friendly with Farley Clement and his wife. I just need some background information, that's all."

"Background? Background on Farley? Background on Leona? What are you talking about?"

"You don't know," Juanita said. She sounded alarmed. "Oh, Jesus, you two don't know."

She examined Connor, then me. "Don't you people watch television? Don't you have a radio? Didn't you hear about Ronald Farron?"

"Ronald Farron? I'm confused," I said.

"Our councilman Ronald Farron. Ronald Farron, about to step up to the national stage! Ronald Farron was killed today."

I felt as if a spear had entered my body at the shoulder and worked its way down my body to my feet.

"Killed how?" Connor had come across to where Juanita was sitting and bent down, the better to hear.

"Tell us," he said. "Please."

"A traffic accident on Highway 230. A head-on collision. Farley Clement and his wife were on the wrong side of the road and drove head on into Ronald Farron's car. I thought you, Eleanor, could give me some information about the Clements. Did they have any kin?"

"I don't know," I said. "I don't think so." I felt small and separate. As though I wasn't there, in the real world, but instead was in some huge space, a huge echoing space. In my mind I saw Farley, dropping the kettle over Farron's picture and saying that it—my hatred of Farron?—would end.

"May I plug my recorder in?" Juanita asked again. Connor got up and put her plug into an outlet near her seat. For the next twenty minutes or so, Connor and I answered questions telling what few facts we knew about Farley and Leona. We left out a lot, of course. Juanita said she did not wish to get into "the twin business," as she termed it. "I just want to focus on the wreck," she said.

I told myself I should be glad she was far from being a serious journalist. A serious journalist might have investigated "the twin business" story more productively than Juanita Star ever could. Even *Crimebeat*, with their skeletal knowledge of the case, knew a good story when they saw one.

"They were quiet people," I said. "Leona had just celebrated her 80th birthday. They had gone on a second honeymoon of sorts."

"And Farley Clement, was he *non compos mentis*?" She made a circle with her finger at her right temple, the universal gesture signifying crazy.

"He most definitely was not," Connor said, his voice stern.

"But he was driving on the wrong side of the road. The police said he drove right into Ronald Farron at high speed on a divided highway." She sounded very sure as she offered this.

"I don't know. I do know he was quite sane," Connor told her.

"He definitely was," I said.

"And the wife?" Juanita asked.

"Leona. The same. Sane. Intelligent. Happy."

"I wonder how something like that can happen," Juanita mused.

"Sometimes the sun can blind you," Connor said. "Have you checked on time of day and the direction they were heading?"

"Excellent," Juanita said. "I'll do just that."

Just then Sadie padded into the room, that disreputable foot in her mouth. Connor and I smiled at each other.

"Well, unless you have anything else to offer, that about sums it up." She yanked the cord that Connor had plugged in and began to coil it up. Sadie dropped the foot and went after the plug as it moved across the floor. "Bad dog!" Juanita said, yanking the cord out of Sadie's reach.

I fetched Juanita's coat and stood at the door. Connor remained seated. Sadie was now on Connor's lap, as if Juanita weren't present at all.

I held back tears. I couldn't bear Juanita knowing how the news of Farley and Leona's death had hit me. But Connor knew. The minute I'd shut the door, he put Sadie back on the floor and came to hold me. For some unknown reason, my mind flashed back to the Lost Pines police station after Brandon Sterling's death. I remembered how upset Janice had been and how Ray had offered her no comfort. That made me cry all the harder.

"So Farley hated Ronald Farron too," Connor said. "Did you know that?" he asked me.

I would tell him the story: Farron's picture, my sudden fury and, of course, the way Farley looked at me before he dropped the tea kettle he'd been holding onto the newspaper. It was his clairvoyance, I was sure.

At the same time, I had the same unnerving thought that I'd had earlier. That if it weren't for Farley's clairvoyance, the boys would still be alive, and Farley and Leona would be too. They were knit together, a sort of death knot.

I didn't want to think that such things existed, and yet I shivered at the very thought of it. A death knot.

CHAPTER TWENTY-TWO

JUNE 13, 2020

The package was on Slick's passenger seat. The instant I saw the lavender tissue, I knew Farley had put it there. I pulled the wrapping off and there it was, the beautiful shawl that Leona had worn just the other night. There was also a note.

My dearest Eleanor. No, Leona does not know my plan. But it was she who suggested passing this wrap to you. I bought it for Leona on our honeymoon. Oddly, we found it at a street fair. The man who sold it to us was African. He was from Mozambique. Like you, Leona was fascinated by the color, the pattern, the weave.

One did not need power beyond the natural to see what you thought of Ronald Farron.. Nonetheless, I allowed mine to intervene. He must be punished for what he did to your friend.

You may wonder if it is fair to take Leona with me. I foresaw how she would react to my death. She would be lost, in pain and she would follow me in death less than a month after my own demise... I am choosing to take Leona with me. She will be with me always.

You, Eleanor, have been a great gift to both of us. Your friendship and Connor's as well. You believed me. The two of you believed and I thank you.

My fingers trembled when I showed the note to Connor. The two of us sat in a stupor, the letter on the table in front of us. I told him my theory, about the death knot. I asked him if we could be part of it.

"A death knot," he said. "Jesus!"

"But look," I started, but he held a finger up to stop me.

"I get it. Believe me, I do," he told me.

We were interrupted by Sadie. She came to Connor's feet, then attempted to lead him into the kitchen so that he could feed her. We both followed the dog, grateful, I think, for her simple, limited needs.

CHAPTER TWENTY-THREE

JUNE 29, 2020

I went alone to talk to Janice Sterling. Connor, the three-person camera crew and Diane would follow in a van. I wasn't eager to do this, but Connor had talked me into it. I drove up in Slick.

I was surprised to see Janice's little red car standing on ground that had once been covered by an aluminum shell. There was no sign of Ray's Escalade.

Without that ugly parking structure, the brick Craftsman regained its architectural due. Did it mean that Ray was gone?

As she ushered me into the living room, Janice seemed to move quickly, her shoulders back. She looked like someone in the military, I thought. *Stand up straight, corporal.* She hadn't seemed that way the other times I'd seen her.

She also had put makeup on. I thought she'd gone a little heavy on the rouge.

"I thought those *Crimebeat* people were coming," she said, "I've already signed the permission form. In fact, I'm looking forward to it. I've sent Sheena copies of the newspaper articles about the boys' surgeries.

I was surprised and my face must have shown it.

"I'll make sure to mention Ray's name, Ray's treatment of the boys once he found out their story."

"You must have loved him once," I said. *He couldn't have been such a jackass then.*

"I must have, but I don't remember anything about that time. All I remember is the way he turned out." Tears welled up in her eyes.

That does happen to people. Did the hatred fall suddenly or slowly? Was there any way to keep it from happening? I tried to change the subject. "Are you planning to stay here?"

"I love this house. My grandfather built it. When he died, my parents moved here. I grew up here."

"You took that aluminum parking thing down."

Janice laughed. "Can you believe this? On our first anniversary, Ray surprised me with it. I thought I'd die when I saw it. but I pretended to be thrilled."

I laughed with her. Then she turned serious. "I wanted the boys to have a father. Is that so wrong?"

Janice and I heard the *Crimebeat* contingent making its way up the driveway. Janice went to the door and opened it. Connor came through first and she recognized him, calling him "Officer Randall."

Meanwhile, the camera man found a chair with a nice background and a side table. He walked across the room and found a picture of the twins when they were about ten. "You have anything more recent?" he asked Janice.

"I'll get you something in a minute," she said. She was being miked and couldn't walk away right then.

A girl crawled around placing lights including one behind Janice. The others were off to each side. She placed another light high and in front of the chair. The room looked a mess, with thick cords going every which way. The girl pulled them flat and began taping them to the floor.

Janice watched, but she didn't seem to mind. The rug, however, was a beautiful oriental with geometrical designs, wool, a Kilim, I thought. I would have objected to the tape, I realized.

"The picture," one of the crew reminded her.

"Oh, yes," she left the room and returned with a picture of the two boys leaping into the air. It was definitely recent. Alex looked exactly as he had when he was in my home. I felt a small sorrow tug at me. Janice must have felt far worse.

Diane said she would be asking the questions, but in the finished product they would drop a narrator in. "We're trying to get Susan Sarandon," she said.

There were two cameras on tripods, one set higher than the other. One man operated both of them. I could see what both cameras were seeing side by side on a computer screen. One showed Janice close up and the other Janice from farther away. The man who had put the microphone on Janice settled down in a corner of the room. He wore big thick earphones.

A chair was pulled up close to Janice. Just as she was about to step over all the things in front of her, Connor asked, "Where should I be? I want to be out of the way."

"I'll answer that," the cameraman piped up. "Go over by the front door. Your girlfriend too." Connor and I scrambled to get out of the way. Then the man with the camera said he'd count down. He told Diane to wait until he called "speed."

Although he kept rolling, he told Janice not to look at the camera. "Look at the girl who is asking the questions," he said, "Look at..."

"Diane," Diane said.

When Janice began talking about the surgeries the twins had

undergone, she started to get up. "No, you don't," the camera man said. "Where are they? We'll bring them in."

The girl who had taped down the wires was dispatched to the dining room to get the newspapers that detailed the operations.

"Tell you what," the camera man said. "Put them there on the hassock and then reach over and pick them up. Hold them up so Diane can see. We'll do an insert later."

When she'd shown the articles, Janice talked about the twins at some length. When she stopped talking, Diane said, "The man who killed your sons died in a car crash recently. Does that give you closure?"

Janice stiffened and looked pained. She covered her face with her hands and bent her upper body down toward her lap. Her shoulders were shaking. When she looked up, she seemed to be begging someone in the room for an answer, "What's the point? Is there a point to all this? How stupid can this be, all of this? Dead, dead, dead. There's no point."

Diane looked at the camera man, wondering what to do. The camera man made a shush sign and we all waited for Janice to shape up again. The camera hadn't been turned off. "I'm sorry," Janice eventually said. She cleared her throat and sniffed. She still fought the spill of tears. The news about Farley had undone her and why not? Why were Alex and Brandon and Farley knotted together in some ugly and unexplainable way?

Although the show was just a half hour long and Janice would be only one of several people who would be interviewed, Diane questioned her for about an hour before the camera man hollered "Cut. We've got it."

To Diane's credit, she put her arm around Janice. "I'm sorry," she said.

"Everybody quiet," the sound guy interjected. "I need some room tone." I tried not to laugh. Room tone. *The room tone is sorrow*, I thought. *Anybody with a brain can see that.*

After this, the camera and lights were trained on the newspaper articles. When that was over, the camera man—I suppose by this time I should have recognized him as the director—wanted a shot of the house from the road.

He left the dismantling of the equipment to the others and went to talk to Janice. He turned into a different person than he'd been throughout the shoot. "Thank you so much. You did great. And by the way, this house, the décor, I like it a lot. That fireplace alone," he said, pointing, "the surround and the hearth, so authentic."

I'd thought of him as an oaf. But I was evidently wrong. He had just been focused on the task at hand, and when that was done, he was gracious, appreciative. When we left the house, Janice was beaming.

"Did you enjoy it?" Connor asked.

"Not enough to watch them photograph the house." I had struggled not to cry when Farley had been mentioned and when Janice lost it. It was so odd, though. A little knot of people pulled together to die.

"I'll tell Diane," he said.

"Do you have to be there for all of the interviews?" I asked.

"No. They wanted us—and I do mean us—so Janice would see faces she knew. That was why we wanted you to go into the house first. They were shocked to learn that Farley and Leona were dead. Diane is going to talk about it as an irony."

"Irony," I said flatly. The right word was 'sacrifice.'

On the way back to Lost Pines, we didn't speak. Unlike traveling with my mother, we weren't listening to the radio. I don't know what Connor thought, but I was trying to sort the way the events of the past year had come out of nowhere and, even more important, how they'd rearranged my life and my future.

I couldn't wait to get a pen and pencil into my hands to draw a timeline.

December 21, 2019 – I see Farley killing Brandon Sterling. Same day I meet Janice and Ray.

December 27, 2019—I drive to Potts and meet Connor. Then I see Alex, Brandon's twin.

Tried as I might, I couldn't put a date on the day Farley had told me about his clairvoyance. I'm usually skeptical of everything, but it didn't occur to me to doubt him. After all, he'd called me by the pet name my parents used: Button.

Oh, the phone. Okay, I pick up Brandon Sterling's cell phone. I can't remember when I watched Farley's attack on the boy on the phone, but even then, I hadn't feared Farley, had I?

At some point, I phone Connor. I wish I could say that he had my trust from the start, but he had as much as I was able to give. Back then, I mean. Now everyone was dead. Farley, Leona. Even Ronald Farron. Some six months after everything began, everything was over or maybe more or less even.

"Nora," Connor said. "You are speeding."

"Sorry," I said, slowing Slick to 65.

We were about to pass the cutoff to the grocery store. "Do we need anything?" I asked.

"Dog food?" he responded.

I laughed. "We have a ton of dog food."

"Well, then. We have everything we need."

I glanced over at him while we waited for the light. He had a cat-who-caught-the-canary look about him. To me, that meant when he said we had everything we needed, he was talking about things more important than groceries.

I put a hand on his thigh and moved it to his knee. He took my hand and held it to his mouth. His lips were slightly open and my fingers caught his breath. Someone behind us leaned on his horn, and I quickly responded, gunning Slick and leaving the honker in the dust.

"That's my girl," Connor said.

"That's right," I answered, happy and proud, gathering speed as we crossed the bridge toward home.

-30-.

ACKNOWLEDGMENTS

Thanks to beta readers Kathleen Hoffman, Bill Spencer, Paula Tremblay, and John Raaf.

ABOUT RUNNING WILD PRESS

Running Wild Press publishes stories that cross genres with great stories and writing. RIZE publishes great genre stories written by people of color and by authors who identify with other marginalized groups. Our team consists of:

Lisa Diane Kastner, Founder and Executive Editor
Joelle Mitchell, Licensing and Strategy Lead
Cody Sisco, Acquisition Editor, RIZE
Benjamin White, Acquisition Editor, Running Wild
Peter A. Wright, Acquisition Editor, Running Wild
Resa Alboher, Editor
Angela Andrews, Editor
Sandra Bush, Editor
Ashley Crantas, Editor
Rebecca Dimyan, Editor
Abigail Efird, Editor
Aimee Hardy, Editor
Henry L. Herz, Editor
Cecilia Kennedy, Editor

Barbara Lockwood, Editor
AE Williams, Editor
Scott Schultz, Editor
Rod Gilley, Editor
Kelly Ottiano, Editor
Carolyn Banks, Editor

Evangeline Estropia, Product Manager
Pulp Art Studios, Cover Design
Standout Books, Interior Design
Polgarus Studios, Interior Design

Learn more about us and our stories at www.runningwildpublishing.com

Loved this story and want more? Follow us at www.runningwildpublishing.com, www.facebook.com/runningwildpress, on Twitter @lisadkastner @RunWildBooks

www.ingramcontent.com/pod-product-compliance
Lightning Source LLC
Chambersburg PA
CBHW051138020726
47501CB00005B/1572

* 9 7 8 1 9 6 3 8 6 9 3 6 1 *